Hard as Nails

It was a trap. The knot in Tucker Flint's gut tightened, and as the realization settled into him, two more gunmen stepped out to face him. That made the odds eight to one. Knowing his own death was imminent and unavoidable, he shifted his thoughts to figuring the best way to take down as many with him as possible. It would mean making his first four shots as rapid as even he was capable.

If he were lucky that would leave four remaining: four whose guns would certainly be sounding his death knell. Only a miracle could save him now. . . .

Hard as Nails

Billy Hall

A Black Horse Western

ROBERT HALE · LONDON

© Billy Hall 2006
First published in Great Britain 2006

ISBN-10: 0-7090-8041-7
ISBN-13: 978-0-7090-8041-1

Robert Hale Limited
Clerkenwell House
Clerkenwell Green
London EC1R 0HT

Typeset by Derek Doyle & Associates, Shaw Heath.
Printed and bound in Great Britain by
Antony Rowe Limited, Wiltshire

CHAPTER 1

Who he was mattered little. What he was needed no explanation.

He rode into town slowly. His right hand rested, almost casually, on his right thigh, inches from the well-worn walnut grips of a Russian .44. Its barrel was short for a Russian. Barely five inches. The end of the barrel, along with the front sight, had been sawn off.

It was not cut roughly. It was clearly done by a gunsmith. The edges were carefully rounded and smoothed, then blued against the relentless attacks of ever-threatening rust. It was fashioned for speed, not accuracy. Short range, large caliber, almost instant death.

On his other hip rode a strikingly different weapon. A Colt Peacemaker .45, with a barrel fully twice the length of the Russian. Its cylinder held five cartridges, instead of six, the one beneath the hammer always being empty. Five rounds, against the Russian's eight. The ninth chamber in the Russian's cylinder also rode empty beneath the hammer.

The Colt was secured with a strap just beneath the

hammer, the slit in its end slid over the button on the holster, to keep it from jarring loose and falling out.

The Russian had no such strap. It was always ready for instant access, at a split second's notice.

It wasn't just the weapons, though. More than their presence, as if the guns were simply part of the man, were his eyes. Wrinkles at the corners indicated endless hours of squinting into the Wyoming sun. Or whatever other territory's sun his profession had led him to wander through. Or perhaps leave hurriedly.

They were flat, those eyes. Pale blue. Devoid of expression or emotion. Restless, never settling on anyone or anything more than an instant, moving constantly. Like a ray of the sun reflected from rippling water, they darted here and there, up ahead, right, left, along the sidewalk, skimming across the edges of the rooftops, scanning windows and doorways, resting for the barest instant on the faces of those who stopped and stared, then moving on in a habitual dance of wariness.

A palpable circle of fear followed him along the dusty street. Nobody could define it, but all sensed the brush of its invisible presence. Some silent breath of violence and death whispered from his aura, menacing, sending tiny shivers up the backs of those who turned to watch him pass.

Quietly, some commented to those closest: 'Gunfighter if I ever saw one.'

'Tough-lookin' fella.'

'S'pose he's another Rafter 2 hand?'

'Could be. Circle J's hirin' gun hands too, I heard.'

'So's the B-bar-C.'

6

'The Mill Iron and U-cross are too.'

'Wonder how come the sheepmen ain't hired any?'

'No money. Gun hands come high. Them sheepmen likely ain't got enough money between 'em to hire even one.'

'That don't give 'em much chance if it comes to a showdown.'

'It'll come to a showdown, all right. No question about that. Only question is when.'

'All the sheepmen got is all them Mexican herders.'

'Just as well have nothin' if it comes to a fight. Most of 'em don't even own a gun. Wouldn't know what to do with it if they had one.'

'That's what worries me. If them sheepmen don't back down, it's gonna come to a range war.'

'Wouldn't be much of a war. Blood-bath'd be more like it. What Mexicans don't get theirselves killed'll get chased clear back to Sonora.'

'I'd put my money on that guy against a dozen o' them Mexes.'

Some of the comments the rider heard. Most he didn't. He ignored them all.

Surprisingly, his face had been carefully shaved. His clothes were cleaner than one would be accustomed to seeing on a cowhand just riding into town. Even his high-crowned hat was clean. No sweat-stains painted the usual pattern of discoloration from the sweat-band two or three inches up the beaver felt. It was an expensive hat, and not old.

The rest of his clothes, though clean, showed a lot

of wear. Except the boots. Most of the boot-shaft was hidden beneath the coarse fabric of his trousers, but the rest showed careful hand-tooling. Precise designs were tooled, then stitched into the leather. They shone as though they were in the habit of receiving a daily coating of bootblack and a polishing-cloth. They alone shifted him out of any possibility of being mistaken for a working cowboy.

Only once did those restless eyes stop. They brushed another set of eyes, then stopped and jerked back. He had no idea why. It was almost as if he recognized something familiar, something that called his name from some place too faint and far away to remember. Some distant tinkling sounded in a hidden recess of his memory for just an instant, forcing his eyes back.

That other set of eyes looked at him as if they, too, felt that faint spark, simultaneously heard that distant chime. Startled more than anything by it, he thought. His gaze paused in its constant survey of his surroundings long enough to take in the rest of her face, then swept down the shapely bodice of her dress, dropped to her feet, and lifted back to her eyes again. They still held their gaze into his. Her beauty nearly left him breathless.

In that instant her gaze tore away from his and made the same quick survey of him that he had executed on her. The results were graphically differ-ent. Her gaze followed with approval the strong, clean-shaven line of his jaw, the cleanliness of his clothes, the broadness of his shoulders, the hard slender torso, then rested briefly on the guns. First one, then the other.

Those probing eyes changed instantly. They turned almost as flat and hard as his own. Her lips abruptly lost the enticing lure of full ripeness. Pressed together, they turned thin and tight, turned down just slightly at the corners. Small, half-circle creases marked each end of her mouth. She turned immediately and walked away.

His lips were even thinner than hers had become, and as empty of expression as the eyes. He was used to the response. He dismissed it instantly. His own lips never lost their thin, hard line across his face, neither smiling nor frowning.

Hers were the only eyes that dared to meet his squarely. Every other set that passed across his face telegraphed the same message to the minds that controlled them. 'Hard.' 'Hardcase.' 'Hard as nails.' As certainly as a hard jerk on a rein, the message always turned those eyes, diverting them to less disturbing vistas.

He rode his horse to the hitch rail in front of a building marked simply 'saLoon.' For the barest instant it appeared he might smile as he glanced at the sign. Nothing pretentious, that was for sure. No 'Spirits Emporium', like the place in Cheyenne, or 'Cow Palace', like the one in Denver. Just 'saLoon,' painted on a rough board in uneven letters. The 'L' was the only capital letter in the word, as though its painter only knew one way to make each letter.

His restless eyes noted one other saloon in town, marked as unpretentiously as this one. It had a larger sign, more neatly lettered, but it, too, bore a single word. It said 'Shorty's'.

Something kindled in him an immediate affinity for the town. Maybe because it was as spare on verbiage as he. Maybe because there was no pretense. Again, like himself. He knew what he was. He made neither excuses nor boasts. He was a hired gun, an instrument of death, for hire. Nothing more. Nothing less.

CHAPTER 2

He stepped from the saddle and flipped the reins around the hitch rail. Without conscious thought he lifted the Russian a couple inches in the holster and dropped it back again twice, ensuring that it rode loose and easy in its readiness.

He closed his eyes for a count of three, then stepped into the dim interior of the saloon as he reopened them. Automatically he took an immediate step sideways and swept the room with ever-restless eyes. They adjusted almost immediately to the lesser light inside because of the three seconds he had kept them closed.

He never thought about it, but he could have turned around and walked out, then given a complete description of the inside of that saloon. He could have described every person present, where they were positioned, including the bartender, where the stove stood, how many tables were spread around the room, and what games were in progress at any of them. He could even have told with uncanny accuracy the weapon each occupant wore, where and how he wore it, and which of the room's denizens would pose the greatest danger in a fight.

It was an ability that set him apart from every other gunman he had ever known. Much of it was a gift, as natural to him as breathing. But he had also carefully nurtured that gift, honing it to razor-edged perfection. It had saved his life more times than he cared to recount.

He stepped to the bar, mentally approving the large mirror behind it. He could survey the room behind him as easily as if he were turned to face it.

'What'll ya have?'

'Whiskey.'

The bartender set a surprisingly clean shot-glass on the bar and filled it. He picked up the coin without comment and moved on. With another sweep of the mirrored images in the bar, the newcomer tossed off the shot.

He stood without breathing for a moment. The harsh liquor washed the dust from his throat and settled in his stomach like a low fire, then began to spread its glow outward, easing the soreness and weariness of too many hours in the saddle.

When the effect of the shot had spread, settled and faded, he turned his back to the bar. He hooked one high heel on the brass rail and fished a sack of Bull Durham out of his shirt pocket. From the same pocket he lifted a packet of cigarette-papers, selected one, and put the rest back.

As the ever restive eyes kept up their scanning of the room he held the paper to make a shallow trough. He carefully filled it with tobacco, grasped the bag's string in his teeth and pulled it tightly shut again. He tucked it back in his pocket, ran his tongue along the edge of the paper, and finished rolling the cigarette. He twisted one end shut and put the other end between his lips, letting it dangle loosely from one corner of his mouth. He fished a match from his pocket, lifted his leg to tighten his pants, struck the match along the back of his thigh, and lighted his smoke, still keeping up his visual surveillance over the flame and the ensuing small cloud of smoke.

He inhaled deeply, then slowly exhaled, savoring once again the calming, soothing spread of the nicotine through his system, just as he had the alcohol.

He knew both were dangerous habits. He never allowed himself more than one shot of whiskey, or one cigarette. Even then he knew they could slow his hand, if ever so slightly. He consoled himself, when he actually thought about it, with the assurance that there was more difference than that in himself and other gunmen anyway. At least there always had been.

Maybe, someday, he'd face somebody for whom that wasn't true. That, too was all right with him. Life had never been something he wanted for too long anyway. Better to die quickly than waste away with consumption or tapeworm or old age.

'Anybody tell me where to find the Flanders ranch?'

His quiet words carried to every corner of the saloon. He might as well have thrown a full fork of manure onto the bar. The room fell silent instantly. Eyes suddenly smoldered, narrowed and focused on him. Jaws clamped. Lips compressed. Conversations

13

stopped in mid-word.

Pregnant silence filled the air, mixing with the smell of beer and whiskey, cigarette smoke and sawdust. Every eye in the place bored into him. Eventually a fifty-something face, wrinkled and toughened by too many harsh Wyoming summers and winters spoke. 'That's a sheep outfit.'

'So I heard.'

'Who are you?'

'Name's Tucker Flint. Most folks just call me Flint. Gets 'em in less trouble than keeping things straight enough to call me Tucker.'

The attempt at humor failed to elicit even a lessening of intensity in the animosity focused on him.

'Whatd'ya want at Flanders?'

'Oh, I wanta find the place, first off. That's why I asked the question.'

A lean, hard-faced man seated at the same table as the speaker started to stand, but was motioned back by the other. He sat back down slowly, but kept his hand on the butt of a pistol he wore like a professional.

'I take it you got business with Flanders?'

'I thought I'd try my hand herdin' sheep. They offered me a job.'

Two dozen pairs of eyes bounced their focus around the room in quick glances. They seemed involved in a sudden dance that infected every set of eyes in the place. It ended as quickly as it began. All eyes swiftly darted back to focus on him. From the corner of his eye Flint saw the bartender edging along the bar.

14

Without turning his head, he addressed him, speaking softly. 'You best stop edgin' closer to that Greener ya got under the bar and start backin' the other way.'

The bartender complied instantly, a little too quickly to keep from appearing awkward in his obedience.

'You don't look much like a sheepherder,' the first speaker observed.

'How do sheepherders look?'

'Like Mexicans er idiots that talk to theirselves, mostly.'

'Well, I ain't Mexican, so I must be an idiot, huh?'

'Did you come in here lookin' to get killed?'

Flint's eyebrows rose. 'The thought hadn't occurred to me, to be real honest. I just stopped in to get a drink an' have a cigarette an' get some directions.'

As he said it, he dropped his cigarette into the sawdust and shifted his weight to grind it out carefully under a boot-heel. It was lost on nobody that the move also put him into a much better position to use his gun, should the need arise.

'This here's the cowman's saloon.'

'Is that so? Then Shorty's must be where the sheepmen shake the dust off?'

The man nodded curtly. 'We don't like drinkin' with people that smell like sheep.'

'Or Mexicans. Or idiots,' the hardcase sitting with the rancher added. 'Or the kind that prefer the company o' sheep to that o' women.'

Flint almost smiled. 'I can understand that.

Nobody's real comfortable drinkin' with people that much better'n him.'

The response was instant. The man stood, sending the chair flying behind him. His gun swept up in a smooth blur too quick to watch. It was rising toward Flint when the roar of the Russian .44 blasted through the room, sending people diving for the floor, scurrying for cover.

The gunman staggered backward. Confusion crossed his face. He stared at the wisp of smoke emanating from the barrel of Flint's pistol, even as it was ripped away by a second streak of fire. He felt that bullet slam into his chest, a scarce inch from the neat round hole already in the front of his shirt. He died before he fell.

His gun level, Flint's eyes darted around the room. 'I didn't ask for that,' he said, his voice calm and steady. 'I'd just as soon not have to kill anyone else.'

The rancher glared at him, red-faced in a mixture of anger and disbelief, but was careful to keep his hands in clear view on the table top. His voice rasped as if it were suddenly difficult for him to speak. 'Do you know who that was?'

'Never had the pleasure.'

'That was Whip Henshaw.'

'You don't say. I've heard of him. I always heard he was greased lightnin' with a gun. I would've expected him to be a whole lot faster.'

'Did Flanders hire you to kill him?'

Keeping his gun level, never stopping his eyes' restless survey of the room, he shook his head. 'Nope. Like I said, I didn't have any idea who he was.

He opened the festivities, I didn't. I just wanted directions to Flanders' place.'

'Why are they hirin' a gunfighter the likes o' you?'

'Maybe because you're hirin' gunfighters the likes o' Henshaw?'

The rancher's face reddened further, but he offered no answer.

Flint knew he needed to get out of that place, and quickly. There were far too many guns in the place, and they were all his enemies, now that they knew he had come to work for the sheep-ranchers.

He slipped the strap from the big Colt Peacemaker and drew it with his left hand. Using both guns to sweep back and forth, he edged toward the door, keeping the room covered as best he could. When he reached the door he stepped through it quickly. He crossed the board sidewalk in two strides, jerked the reins loose from the hitch rail, stepped into the saddle and backed his horse down the street, keeping the front door of the saloon under constant surveillance. Only when he reached the hitch rail in front of Shorty's did he dismount.

Even then, he kept the horse between himself and the other saloon until he had secured the reins to that hitch rail. Then he holstered his weapons and swiftly strode into the second saloon he had entered that day.

CHAPTER 3

The atmosphere of Shorty's was markedly different. 'Cantina,' Flint silently told himself as he entered.

Those within numbered almost equally Mexican and Caucasian. On a stage near the back of the room a guitar played while a couple danced. The dance was lively, rollicking, exuberant. A half-circle of men stood watching, grinning openly. Some clapped or tapped soft leather shoes in time to the music.

Flint had only an instant to survey the room. He was accosted just inside the door by a pair of husky Mexicans. Each had a large knife conspicuously sheathed at his belt. Either looked capable of ripping him in two bare-handed, if necessary.

'What is your business here, *señor?*' one asked quietly.

'*Estoy buscando el jefe del rancho de Flanders.*'

A small flicker of surprise crossed both pairs of eyes, but their demeanor did not change. They ignored the implied invitation to converse in Spanish, responding instead in English.

'And just what is your business with Señor Flanders?'

18

Irritation welled abruptly in Flint. His pale-blue eyes went flat and hard. His words remained soft, but they were crisp and brittle. 'I'll bother to answer that question just to avoid takin' them knives you're wearin' and shovin' 'em up through your chins till they come out the top o' your heads.'

The two bristled and dropped their hands to the knife-handles. They never saw him reach for either gun. One instant they were confronting a single cowboy, confident in their strength and ability. The next each stared at the muzzle of a pistol less than two inches from his nose.

'I don't aim to stand here and answer any more questions than that. My business is with Flanders, not you two. My name is Tucker Flint.'

When he spit out his name, their demeanor changed swiftly. Their hands moved away from the knife handles as if they were suddenly too hot to touch. They kept both hands awkwardly away from their bodies, fingers splayed wide. 'My apologies, Señor Flint,' one said a little too quickly. 'We did not know. I will tell Señor Flanders you have arrived.'

He hurried away, leaving the other to look uncomfortable and frightened. 'You had a good trip here, Señor Flint?' he offered.

Flint didn't bother to answer. He smoothly slid both guns back into their holsters as he continued the ever constant scanning of the saloon's patrons. The ill-prepared guard's face betrayed a rush of relief when his companion returned almost immediately. 'Please, Señor Flint, I will take you to Señor Flanders,' he said.

Flint nodded and followed the pair. As they approached a table well removed from the stage, a man in his late thirties or early forties stood and extended his hand. 'Tucker Flint? I'm Ian Flanders. I can't tell you how glad I am to see you.'

The warmth of the grip Flint returned was belied by his dry words. 'I didn't get that impression from the welcome committee.'

Rather than apologize, Flanders grinned. 'Symptom of the times, I'm afraid. We're more'n a little jumpy.'

He waved a nonchalant hand at others at the table. 'This here's Les O'Havre. Jack Conners. Will Stout. Fred Leason. It's the five of us, along with Betty Burton who scraped up the money to hire you. Have any trouble gettin' here?'

'Not till I hit town.'

Flanders' eyebrows, along with four other sets around the table, rose. 'You had trouble in town already?'

Flint shrugged. 'The fellas you sent to hire me didn't bother tellin' me there was two saloons in town, and I oughta not go blunderin' into the wrong one.'

Flanders' eyes showed sudden concern. 'You stopped at Bub's place?'

'If that's the name of the other saloon, then I guess you could say that. When I asked for directions to your place it sorta had the effect o' tossin' a skunk out in the middle o' the room.'

'I can believe that! I'm surprised you got out in one piece.'

'I did. They got one less gunfighter than they had this mornin', though.'

'Somebody tried to kill you?'

Flint nodded again. 'Guy named Henshaw.'

Flanders' eyes widened. The others leaned back in their chairs, as if a little more room would make what he was about to say easier to hear. 'Whip Henshaw pulled a gun on you? How in Sam Hill did you talk him out of killing you?'

'I didn't. He was just way too slow. I shot 'im.'

The five men looked at one another, their jaws unwittingly hanging open. It was Les O'Havre who found his voice first. 'Whip Henshaw went for his gun first, and you beat him to the draw? I watched that man kill one of my herders. He was so fast I never even seen him reach for that gun. You outdrew him?'

'I'm here. He ain't.'

Flanders found his voice again. 'Well! That didn't take long. I really didn't expect anything to start happening that quick. Well. Well, I guess you've already earned the up-front bonus money. To be honest, most of us weren't happy about handin' over five hundred dollars to a total stranger, just to get you to show up. Odds were runnin' just about even you'd never show.'

Flint almost smiled. 'Only even? I'd have expected two to one at least.'

'Which way?' Jack Conners inserted.

'Against,' Flint responded immediately. 'Gunfighters ain't noted for bein' honorable gentle-men.'

21

'But you are?'

'I'm a man of my word. If I was goin' to sell my integrity, it wouldn't be for five hundred dollars.'

'How much would it take?' Fred Leason asked over the rim of his beer-glass.

A tiny smile rippled at the corners of Flint's mouth as he answered. 'I don't know. I figured if I was ever goin' to do that, it'd have to be so much money that every time my conscience kicked up I could just plumb bury it with money.'

'That'd take a lot of money.'

'More'n I've run across yet anyway,' Flint agreed. 'How many other hands do you have that can use a gun?'

The five exchanged glances, but none seemed willing to answer the question.

Flint's eyes bored into Flanders, demanding an answer. Flanders cleared his throat. Conners shifted on his chair. Leason took off his hat, ran his hand through his hair and replaced the hat. It was Will Stout who eventually dared answer the question: 'You're it, Flint.'

Fire flashed briefly in Flint's eyes. 'I'm it? Just me? You hired me to take on the cattlemen, all by myself? And you didn't bother to tell me that?'

It was, again, Stout who faced up to the situation. 'I'll admit that wasn't fair, and some less than honest,' he said. 'The truth is, we ain't got the kind o' money the cattlemen have. We're all just startin' out. Hump Burton was the only one that wasn't startin' on a shoestring, and he went an' got himself killed pertneart a year ago. We pooled our money just to hire you. Fact is, we'd love to hire fifteen or twenty if we could.'

Conners chimed in: 'Mind you, we ain't askin' you to take on the whole bunch o' the cattlemen all by yourself. We need your know-how. We ain't got no idea how to stand up to the toughs they been bringin' in. There ain't a whole lot o' law in this territory yet. There's a county sheriff but he's an old cowboy that's rode for half the ranchers an' hates sheep.'

'We're willing to do the fighting, if it comes to that,' Leason agreed. 'You just gotta show us how and when and where.'

'And just what do you intend to fight with?' Flint demanded.

Flanders bristled visibly. 'We ain't a bunch o' pansies, Flint! We've fought our share o' battles. We was all in the war, an' did our share o' killin'. In spite o' what the ranchers think, raisin' sheep ain't a job for weaklin's or the faint o' heart. You'll find we're tough enough. But fightin' a bunch o' ranchers with hired gun hands ain't the same. We gotta have a general leadin' the fight, or some right good advice on how to lead it. We hired you for what you know 'bout fightin' range wars, not so's you can go fight it all by yourself.'

The absurdity of the situation stretched Flint's credulity beyond its limits. He probed the faces peering intently back at him, waiting for some crazy punch line, waiting for some indication that this was an elaborate hoax to test his mettle. What he saw instead was a quiet desperation. He realized with a rush that they were telling him the simple truth. They had pooled their resources, scraped together all the spare cash they could between them, and come up with just enough to pay him the up-front money he demanded and guarantee three months' wages, at one hundred dollars a month. That was it. He was their last, best hope. They had pinned it all on him.

He knew, without even thinking about it, what he would do. Integrity required him to give back the five hundred dollars. Even an ounce of common sense required him to walk out of here, get on his horse, ride away and never look back. To think of any alternative was absolutely crazy.

He framed the words in his mind. Words to scorch their ears and reduce them to shame and embarrassment came easily. With an effort, he replaced them with words expressing his reluctance to commit suicide for any price. Still unspoken, he carefully inserted words of apology that he absolutely couldn't accept such a proposition.

'You gotta be nuts!' poured out of his mouth instead.

Nothing changed in the pleading of their stares. Flanders alone responded. He bobbed his head once in agreement. 'I 'spect we are. But desperate is more like it. I ain't never had to say such a thing in my life, but that's what it is. We're desperate. We asked around, and pertneart everybody we asked said you was the best there ever was. We knew we couldn't hire more'n one, so we figured we'd better get the best. And that's where it's at. It's you that gives us some

24

glimmer o' hope, or else we just ain't got none. That's just where it's at.'

'You gotta be nuts,' Flint heard himself repeating.

Flanders leaned back. 'Well, we're bein' straight with you. If you choose, you can walk outa here and ride away. We wouldn't even ask for the up-front money back, an' we'd not think ill of you. We understand what we're asking. But you gotta know, you're our last hope.'

Twice Flint tensed his muscles to turn and walk away. Twice he looked again into the half-circle of eyes that bored into his own. He saw something in them he didn't want to look at or think about.

He saw years of hard work and dire peril that had been invested in the dream of owning a piece of ground and livestock to make it pay. He saw the heartbreak of failed efforts and lost battles, as well as lost friends and family members. He saw the weariness of fighting the burning sun in summer and bone-chilling blizzards every winter. He saw the persistence of those who slogged ahead against all odds, sloughing off their fatigue and discouragement, all just to carve out a little piece of earth they could call their own. He saw the hopes and dreams of being able to hand that piece of earth on to children, and maybe even live to bounce grandchildren on aged and aching knees. He saw it all hinging squarely on his ability to do the impossible, to accept the ridiculous, to attempt the absurd.

He had been in enough range squabbles and personal feuds to know that dreams and hopes don't win battles. He understood that the good people didn't somehow win because they were good. In fact, they were usually the losers. Those without scruples or consciences forged ahead while those with morals and integrity hesitated. He'd watched it happen too many times to hold any illusions that this time could be any different. Staying alive in his business meant being sure you were on the side with the best odds going in.

Still, he had accepted their money. He had shaken the hand of their messenger. He had taken the five hundred dollars. He wondered suddenly how many sheep some of them had sold below market price to come up with their share. But if he handed back the money, he'd be even. He hadn't agreed to suicide.

On the other hand, he had accepted the money. That meant he gave his word. He didn't just give his word to show up and look the situation over. He had accepted the commitment to do the job. He hadn't stipulated any conditions. He hadn't thought to ask the right questions.

'Where's Howard Montague? The guy that looked me up in Tucson?'

'Dead,' Flanders replied. 'Shot by a Circle J gunman the day after he got back.'

Flint took a deep breath. 'How many hands do you have?'

The four men exchanged looks, sudden hope blossoming in every set of eyes. 'Herders?' Flanders asked.

Flint nodded silently.

'Well, I got nine.'

'I got eleven,' Stout offered.

26

'Five, counting the campjacks,' from Conners.

'Eight,' from Leason.

'Just four, and one old campjack pertneart as bad off as Herman,' O'Havre added.

'Mrs Burton has ten or twelve,' Flanders concluded. 'She's got the biggest spread and the most sheep. She's the only one that ain't on such a ragged shoestring.'

'Forty-seven,' Flint tallied. 'That ain't bad. How many hands would the ranchers add up to?'

'Gun hands or cowboys?'

'Both.'

The five thought silently for a long moment. It was O'Havre who responded first. 'I'd say close to sixty regular hands. The last I knew the hired gunmen would probably add up to twenty at least.'

The others nodded. 'That's close,' Leason agreed.

The odds weren't as bad as he'd expected. Not quite two to one against them. 'How many of your herders can handle a gun?'

The five men suddenly became intent on examining the table top, or their fingernails, or the ceiling. Again, it was O'Havre who put their hesitancy into words. 'Maybe a dozen, tops.'

Flint's eyebrows flew up. 'A dozen?'

O'Havre shrugged. 'Look around. How many guns do you see worn in here?'

'Four, besides you five,' Flint answered instantly. 'Mostly knives.'

O'Havre nodded. 'And how many of the four are white?'

Again, Flint's ability to assess instantly and remember details asserted itself with no hesitation. 'All four.'

'Out of that forty-seven hands, counting herders, campjacks and flunkees, we got maybe ten white men. The rest are Mexicans. They grew up poor as dirt in Mexico. They came up here because twenty dollars a month is big money. Most of 'em have never touched a gun, let alone owned one or known how to use it.'

As the words soaked in, Flint knew with absolute certainty it was time to bail out and ride away. If he didn't, he'd just be telling Howard Montague to move over to make room for him in the graveyard.

CHAPTER 4

They waited patiently. One leaned against the wall, leisurely smoking a cigarette. The other lounged against a post that supported the sloped roof over the sidewalk.

Flint stepped out the door of Shorty's, squinting at the brightness of the sun. He spotted the two instantly, but chose to ignore them. He started toward his horse.

The voice stopped him half-way there. 'Ya think we'll go away if ya pretend ya don't see us?'

He looked squarely at them then. He didn't need to notice the guns tied down low on their thighs. He didn't need to appraise them as cowboys or gunmen. He had done that with the instinctive quick glance as he had walked out of Shorty's.

'You might want to do that,' he responded.

As if pulled by the same magnet, both straightened and stepped into the street. 'An' let ya off the hook?' the first speaker asked.

Someone in Shorty's had noticed the exchange. Half a dozen herders and two of the sheep-ranchers slid out of the door and sidled along the front of the building, where they could see without being mistaken for participants in the coming action.

'Haven't felt that hook,' Flint responded. 'I only just heard the line.'

Ignoring the pun, the speaker of the duo said: 'Tell ya what, Flint. Since we're in a purty good mood today, we'll give ya one chance to git back on that there horse an' ride out. This here country ain't healthy fer anyone that'll work fer sheepmen.'

'Generous of you,' Flint said, squaring himself and walking several steps toward the approaching gunmen. 'I guess I could offer you boys the same deal.'

One quick glance darted between the two gunmen. The speaker said: 'Then I guess we gotta do this.'

As if on signal, both of their guns leaped into their hands. The roar of two shots echoed off the false-fronts of stores that lined the narrow streets. Both gunmen halted the rise of their weapons just short of pointing toward Flint. Two more shots, spaced a split second further apart chased the echoes of the first two.

The Russian .44 in Flint's hand trailed a wisp of smoke upward.

The batwing doors of the saLoon burst open, emitting a gunman with a double-barreled shotgun to his shoulder, pointing directly at Flint.

The .44 in Flint's hand bucked and barked three times in such rapid succession that the echoes mingled together into a single roar. The shotgun roared harmlessly into the air as its bearer was blown back into the saLoon.

The lifeless bodies of all three gunmen settled onto ground and sawdust at almost the same time. Deathly hush settled with them, enveloping the street in a moment of breathless stupor.

The spell was broken by the woman whose eyes Flint had met on his way into town. She lunged out the door of Steinberg's Mercantile Store. Her eyes swept up and down the street, focusing briefly on each of the gunmen, then the pair of boots protruding, toes skyward, from the door of the saLoon.

For the second time Flint felt, rather than saw, the eyes focus on him. He chanced to interrupt his careful watch of the door of the saLoon long enough to meet her gaze briefly. He wasn't sure whether the fire that flared there was triumph or animosity.

'What happened?' she demanded.

Ian Flanders responded from the sidewalk in front of Shorty's. 'Two of the ranchers' hired guns thought they'd get rid o' Flint straight away. They was waitin' when he come out. They wasn't nowheres near fast enough.'

'The other one thought he'd try usin' the barkeep's shotgun,' Flint followed.

One of the Mexican herders who had come outside to watch spoke then. 'Señor Flint, I am confuse how you do that. I hear you shoot seven times. I count them. Bang, bang. Bang, bang. Then bang, bang, bang. *Uno, dos. Tres, cuatro. Cinco, seis, siete.* How do you make a six-shooter shoot seven times?'

31

A trace of smile passed for just an instant across Flint's mouth. Still watching the front door of the saLoon, he began ejecting spent brass and reloading the Russian from the loops on his belt. 'It's a Russian,' he explained. 'Nine-shot. Sorta heavy, but the extras are handy sometimes.'

'Who started this?' the woman demanded.

'They did, Betty,' Flanders offered. 'I guess you folks ain't been introduced proper yet. Flint, this here's Mrs Burton. Betty, this's Flint Tucker. The one we sent for.'

Flint nodded curtly without speaking.

Her eyes surveyed him as though seeing him for the first time. To Flanders, rather than to Flint, she said: 'I saw him ride into town. I have to admit, I'm rather glad he's on our side.'

She turned to Flint, speaking directly to him for the first time. 'Mr Tucker, why do you suppose three of the ranchers' gunmen would accost you so soon upon your arrival here?'

Flint glanced at her then immediately resumed his watchfulness. Instead of answering, he said: 'We'd best be movin' outa the street. Someone could be standin' back in the saLoon where we can't see, aimin'a rifle at us right now.'

He started to turn back to Shorty's, to continue the conversation there. Abruptly he realized it was unlikely that Mrs Burton would set foot within the place. Few respectable women would even consider doing so.

Mentally he shrugged. *Her problem*, he told himself silently.

Glancing back toward the door of the ranchers' hang-out, she followed Flint into Shorty's with no discernible hesitation. It seemed to surprise nobody except Flint. She walked in and sat down at a table close to the door, dropping her handbag on the sawdust-covered floor. The tiniest flicker of a smile glimmered briefly in her eyes as she saw Flint's obvious discomfiture with her presence there. Briskly she said: 'I would ask the question again, Mr Flint. Why do you suppose three of the ranchers' gunmen would accost you so soon upon your arrival?'

Flint took off his hat and regained his composure, hoping she hadn't noticed the crack in his brittle exterior which he had allowed for that instant. Even as the thought flashed through his mind, it fired a spark of resentment and irritation that she had done so. That gave an edge to his voice as he responded: 'Ask them.'

Her lips compressed slightly. The half-circle creases at each end of her mouth were instantly back in place. 'I had hoped you might be a little more able to offer an answer than they. I suspect they are decidedly unlikely to tell me anything.'

Flanders stepped in to try rescue the situation, or at least to keep it from deteriorating further. 'Flint stopped at the wrong saloon first. He asked for directions to my place. Whip Henshaw went for his gun. Flint shot him.'

Her eyes darted back to Flint. 'You outdrew Whip Henshaw?'

'I'm here.'

'Then you have already killed four of their gunfighters, when you've been in town less than two hours?'

He looked at her, not bothering to answer.

'That's a fact,' Les O'Havre hurried to offer. 'We sure enough got the right man for the job, I'd have to say. I've never seen anything like it. Those two outside were faster with their guns than anyone I've ever seen. And Flint shot 'em both before they could get off a shot.' He shook his head. 'Didn't get off a shot.'

Betty Burton took a deep breath. 'I suppose I ought not to be upset at that. That is, after all, what we hired you for.'

'We didn't expect things to start happenin' so fast, is all,' Ian Flanders voiced what they were all thinking.

'So what is your plan, Mr Tucker?' Betty turned the conversation back to her desired direction.

'He knows he's our only gun hand,' Will Stout informed her.

'And you're still here,' Betty said, rather than asked. 'I have to admit, that does surprise me some. Why?'

Flint resisted the effort to smile at the question. His eyes bored relentlessly into hers. 'Tucker's my first name. Usin' it with a "mister" seems sorta wrong. Folks just call me Flint. But to answer your question, I took your money.'

'You could always give it back.'

'That'd be all right with you?'

'It would be within your rights. After all, we weren't exactly honest with you up front. We didn't

34

bother to tell you that you were the only one we could hire. If you chose to do that, there isn't a lot we could do about it.'

'I ain't in the habit o' breakin' my word.'

Twice she acted as if to answer, and each time closed her mouth. When she did speak, there was a very slight lessening of the edge on her voice. 'Then what is your plan?'

A brief pause before he answered left Flint feeling as if everyone at the table, and at a second table that had been dragged over close, were holding their collective breath for his answer. 'First thing we gotta do is get some more guns on our side.'

'And how would you suggest we do that? I believe you have already been informed that you are the only gunfighter we can afford to hire.'

'We gotta teach your herders to use a gun.'

Her eyebrows arched. 'The Mexicans?'

'That's who you got.'

'And how do you intend to teach them to do that? How long would it take to make gunfighters out of them?'

He shook his head. 'Not gunfighters. Riflemen. It don't take all that long for people to learn to use a rifle. A little teachin', a little practice, an' they can hold their own, if they ain't out in the open.'

'But none of them even owns a rifle.'

'Get 'em some.'

'Rifles are expensive, Flint. 'I was lookin' at one o' them new Winchester 73s over at Steinberg's just yesterday. Fifty-two dollars apiece. That's without no ammunition.'

'How much are your ranches worth?' Flint countered.

Silence descended abruptly. It was broken after some moments by Betty. 'He's right. It's not right to ask these men to herd our sheep if we won't even give them the means to defend themselves. We can start with half a dozen of the rifles. Amos will probably have that many in stock.'

'It'll take a couple hundred rounds o' ammunition for each one,' Flint added.

Betty hesitated, obviously adding up the cost in her head. 'Very well.'

'One more thing,' Flint said, holding up a hand.

'Yes?'

'The herders gotta know there's a reason for 'em learnin' ta shoot. The ones that learn good enough gotta get ta keep their rifle.'

The sound of half a dozen throats emitting something akin to a hoarse wheeze all at once almost made him laugh. Jack Conners, his voice rising half an octave above its usual pitch, said: 'You want us to give them Mexes a Winchester 73? That's worth three months' o' their wages.'

'Three months wages for a herder ain't much for puttin' your life on the line,' Flint argued. 'If there ain't nothin' in it for 'em, they ain't gonna do it. If they know they'll get their own rifle if they're good, they'll learn real quick.'

Ian Flanders, who always seemed to reason more swiftly than the rest, spoke up. 'I'd be all for that on one condition. The rifles belong to the ones that use 'em well, an' stay with us all the way through this thing. If they run out in the middle o' the fight, they go empty-handed.'

At least it was a plan to start with. Suicide probably, but a plan.

CHAPTER 5

He reined in sharply. He slid from the saddle, looking around in all directions. He moved around his horse slowly, using the horse for cover. Even as he did so, he knew it was unlikely that the horse would provide any protection. He had no idea where the object of his search might be.

Mentally he brought up a panorama of the land around the Burton sheep ranch. He paid special mind to every high spot he had noted, especially those that were in direct line of sight from the ranch buildings.

He looked again at the other horse. It was tied to a clump of brush in a small hollow. Flint knew cowboys. Its rider wouldn't have left the horse very far from where he was. Cowboys never walked further than absolutely necessary.

The nearest of the high points that might be the rider's destination was probably 300 yards up the ridge. Moving as silently as possible, Flint edged in that direction. He eased the big Colt .45 Peacemaker from its butt forward, left-side holster. He sidled up the hill, watching intently.

As he approached the crest of the hill he dropped to all fours, being careful to keep the end of the pistol's barrel clear of the ground. At the very crest, he slid forward on his stomach, watching, listening.

He lay in the tall grass, peering about intently. Then a movement caught his eye and he focused on it instantly.

Fifty yards in front of him, barely visible in the grass, a man lay stretched on the ground. He held a telescope, pointed toward the buildings of the Burton ranch.

Several things ran through Flint's mind. *Too far away to be tryin' ta pick anybody off. Ain't even got his rifle. Left it on his horse. Tryin' ta see what we're up to.*

That the man was one of the ranchers' hired gun hands there was little doubt. What he should do at this point was less clear. He could easily shoot him from here, with the Peacemaker. Even though he was a hired gun hand, the thought of cold-bloodedly shooting someone in the back was repulsive to him.

He could work closer, then challenge the man to stand up and draw against him or surrender. If he chose to surrender, what would he do with him? There was no place on the Burton ranch in which to confine a prisoner. If he took him all the way to the county seat to a jail, what would he charge him with? It probably wasn't against the law to watch somebody's ranch with a telescope.

On the other hand, he couldn't just let him continue his surveillance. He didn't want the ranchers to know what he was up to. Surprise was the only thing that might give the herders a chance against the greater numbers of better-armed and better-skilled gunfighters and cowboys who rode for the cattle brands.

Slowly he eased backward, making as little noise as possible. When he was well below the brow of the hill and sure that the hidden watcher could not see him, he rose and walked quickly to his horse. *Gotta be twelve or fourteen miles to the nearest cow ranch*, he told himself silently. *He won't dare stop at no sheep ranch.*

He mounted his horse and rode to the tethered mount of the ranchers' spy. Sliding the Colt Peacemaker from his holster, he looked at the saddled horse. In his mind he made an imaginary X from the animal's eyes to his ears. The Peacemaker pointed and roared. A neat round hole appeared exactly in the center of the mental X he had made on the animal's face.

The horse dropped instantly. The sound of the .45 bounced off the surrounding hills. Before the echoes died, Flint was riding away at a brisk trot. A tight smile played briefly around the corners of his mouth.

Betty Burton watched anxiously from the porch of the house as he rode into the yard. She stepped into the barn before he could finish unsaddling his horse. 'I heard a shot.'

'Yes ma'am.'

'Was that you?'

'Yes ma'am.'

Trying to hide her exasperation she said: 'Did you shoot somebody?'

'No ma'am.'

She folded her arms, staring at him with smoldering eyes. He dropped the saddle on an empty tree, rubbed the horse down and dumped half a gallon of oats into the feed-trough at the front of the stall. Only then did he address the ranch's owner.

'There was one o' the rancher's guys watchin' the place from the ridge yonder.'

She tried without complete success to stifle the gasp that sought to escape her lips. 'The west ridge?'

'Yes ma'am.'

'Why? He couldn't possibly shoot anybody from there. It's too far.'

'Yes ma'am. He didn't aim ta shoot nobody. He was just watchin'. Had a telescope.'

Her brow furrowed in confusion. 'Just watching? Why?'

'Tryin' ta figure out what we're up to, likely. They ain't heard nothin' from us since the day I got here. They're likely hirin' more gun hands. They gotta be wonderin' what we're up to. So I 'spect they sent that fella ta find out.'

'And you— No. You said you didn't shoot him. But I heard a shot.'

'I shot his horse.'

This time the gasp escaped unobstructed. 'You what?'

'I shot his horse. He left 'im tied to a bush whilst he lay out on the ridge, watchin'.'

'Why in the world would you shoot his horse?'

She thought he was going to smile for an instant. He didn't. As expressionless as ever he said: 'It's a long way back ta any o' the ranches. He won't dare hoof it inta any sheep outfit ta try ta git another

41

horse. I just sorta thought it'd be fittin' that he should walk home.'

She thought about it for a long moment. 'It's upwards of fourteen miles to the closest cattle ranch.'

'That's 'bout what I figgered.'

'That's a terribly long walk.'

'He'll be some sore all right. He likely ain't used ta ridin' shank's mares atall, let alone that far. Walkin' that far wearin' ridin' boots'll likely lame 'im up for a month er two.'

'Fourteen miles!' she breathed.

He nodded. 'Ain't just walkin'. He don't dare leave 'is saddle'n bridle there. He'll figger they're gone for good if he does. So he'll have ta get the saddle pulled out from under the dead horse, an' then sling it up on his shoulder an' carry it an' the bridle the whole way, too.'

A smile played briefly around her mouth, then disappeared. 'But you shot that poor horse!'

'Yes ma'am.'

'Couldn't you have just, just, I don't know. Couldn't you have just brought the horse here?'

'No ma'am. I think they call that horse-stealin'.'

'Well, you could have unsaddled it and turned it loose. Let him try to catch it.'

'Yeah, an' just my luck it'd be a trained horse, an' he'da whistled for it an' it'da come a-runnin'.'

'But, but you didn't have to kill the poor thing.'

She forced herself to keep from shuddering at the icy absence of emotion in his stare. 'I've shot a lot o' things, ma'am. I ain't likely ta lose sleep over a horse.'

With that he walked from the barn, leaving her standing, at a loss for words.

A few minutes later she heard the regularly spaced reports of the Winchester .44-40 rifles from the target range he had set up behind the bunkhouse.

CHAPTER 6

'This ain't cow country.'

The three riders jerked their mounts to a halt. Almost as one they wheeled them to face him. Flint stood beside a tall clump of thick brush which they had just ridden past. The trail they were following led directly to the Burton sheep ranch.

Beside him stood one of the Mexicans who had stopped him as he entered Shorty's saloon in town that first day. He held a Winchester Model 73 loosely in his left hand. Almost absent-mindedly Flint noted the error. He could expect no help from Amado Martinez. By the time he shifted the rifle to his right hand and lifted it, any gunplay would already be over.

'You boys lookin' for somethin' in partic'lar?'

The three eased their horses apart, giving them room to draw their weapons and fire without getting in each other's way.

'You kilt my horse,' one of them gritted.

'How's your feet?' Flint asked amiably.

One of the other gunmen snorted a brief laugh, cut short by the quick glare from the first speaker. 'That was my best horse,' the other continued.

'You shouldn'ta been crawlin' around on your belly in the middle o' sheep country then. Somebody might mistake you for a rattlesnake.'

'I go where I want and do what I want.'

'Not around here you won't.'

'Yeah? Who's gonna stop me?'

'Me.'

That seemed to be a signal. Four hands darted to well-used gun butts. Four pistols were jerked from their holsters.

Flint's gun barked before any of them had a gun clear of leather. One of the gunmen jerked his hands skyward and flopped backward, hit the cantle of his saddle and rolled off sideways to the ground.

Long before he even contacted that cantle, Flint's gun barked a second time. The second gunman, his gun clear of leather, just lifting to center on his adversary, never lived to know he had failed. A hot lead projectile from Flint's Russian .44 shattered his heart.

At almost the same instant as that bullet contacted the man's shirt, Flint's gun barrel had already swung, even as Flint crouched in hopes of the third gunman firing high.

Flint didn't squeeze the trigger. He stared in confusion. The third gunman, strangling, gurgling sounds escaping his lips, was clawing at the handle of a knife protruding from the front of his throat. As he tried, twin fountains of blood blossomed, one from his throat, the other from his mouth. The two crimson fountains combined to form a single spout of blood that covered the pommel of his saddle. His gun slid from his fingers to the ground. He silently followed it scarcely two seconds later.

Flint looked to his right. Amado still stood with the Winchester held loosely in his left hand. The knife-sheath at his belt was empty. Flint willed himself not to shudder.

'I think we have reduced the enemy by a little bit,' Amado observed.

'*Gracias*,' Flint responded. 'I never seen anybody handle a knife that fast.'

Amado grinned broadly. 'I thought I might just watch to see if you are really so fast to kill three gunfighters all by yourself. Then I think: "No, I am not yet good enough with the rifle to let my teacher get himself killed." So I decide maybe I can make it only two that you must take care of.'

'Let's tie 'em over their saddles an' send 'em home,' Flint said instead of answering.

He marveled at the ease with which the big Mexican picked up the lifeless bodies and heaved them across their saddles. Silently grateful, he used each of the dead men's lariats to tie them in place.

'Señor Flint,' Amado objected, 'if you are careful, you could tie all three of them with only one of the riatas. Then I could have one of the riatas for my very own.'

Flint shook his head. 'I don't take nothin' off folks I have ta kill.'

'But Señor,' Amado argued, 'they do not need them any more. And they will probably have enough gold in their pockets for me to buy my very own rifle, and maybe a pistol too, that you can teach me to use.'

Flint turned to face the man squarely. 'Amado, I ain't a thief. I'll not have it said I looked for an excuse ta kill someone so I could take somethin' o' his.'

'But these mens, they will be taken by their horses back to one of the ranches. They do not have families there. They are gunfighters. *Bandidos.* Who will get the money from their pockets? They will not bury their money with them. Should not we make use of that money instead of some of the others that want to kill us?'

Flint ignored the argument. His voice turned hard and flat. 'Just tie the reins up to their saddle horns.'

Amado acted as if he intended to argue further, then he shrugged. He did as he was told. Then he took the knife he had removed from the one gunman's throat and carefully cleaned and dried the blade, replacing it in the sheath at his belt.

Flint slapped each of the horses smartly on the rump with his hat. Already edgy from the noise of the gunfire and the smell of blood, all three horses bolted, galloping away in a cloud of dust.

'I do not understand you, Señor Flint,' Amado muttered as they returned to their own horses. 'You are a strange gringo. A very strange gringo. Hard, and very, very good with a gun. But very strange.'

Having finished the watchful circle around the ranch, the two returned to the barn and put their horses away. Betty met them as they left the building. He noticed with approval the rifle that she carried with her, even here in her own yard. 'I thought I heard shooting.'

47

He nodded. 'The fella I left on foot the other day came back. He brought a couple of his friends with him.'

She worked unsuccessfully to hide her alarm. 'Three of them. Here?'

'They was headin' here. We spotted 'em, an' sorta spoiled their party.'

'Señor Flint, he is very, very fast with that gun,' Amado said.

Betty scarcely looked at him. 'You killed them?'

He nodded again. 'Two of 'em. Amado took care of one.'

This time her gaze turned fully on him. She looked at him with obvious amazement. 'You did, Amado?'

'*Sí, señora.*'

'With the rifle?'

'No, *señora.* I am not yet good enough to try to use it in a time such as that. No, *señora,* I put my knife in his throat so Señor Flint can only worry about two at a time.'

'So you killed two more men,' she repeated, staring accusingly at Flint.

'They was nothin' but hired guns, just like me.'

'But you deliberately baited them. You saw them coming. You almost forced them to draw on you. Just so you could kill them.'

'That's my job.'

'And it doesn't even bother you?'

'Why should it bother me? Like I said, it's my job.'

'It's your job to have no morals, no compunctions about murder?'

48

'Now wait a minute! I didn't say I had no morals. I do what I think's right.'

'You think it's right to kill people?'

'People that need to be killed, sure. Like I keep sayin', it's my job.'

'And that's not immoral to you?'

'Not if I'm doin' what I'm paid to do. Providin' they got it comin', that is. I don't go killin' folks that ain't got it comin', or ain't involved somehow.'

'And that makes it moral?'

'Does to me. When I hire out to someone to do a job, I do the job I was hired to do. I do it the best and fastest way I can find to do it. In this here situation, that means I gotta kill off as many o' their gunfighters as I can. They got a slew of 'em. There's only one o' me.'

'So if that's all there is to it, why don't you just lie up in the rocks somewhere and pick them off with your rifle, like shooting buffalo?'

He frowned. 'Well, there's two reasons. One is, that ain't right. That'd be murder. To not give the other guy a chance, I mean. I always give the other guy a fair shake. I ain't never shot nobody in the back, or nobody that didn't have a chance to shoot me instead. Every man I face can either grab for his gun or walk away. It's his choice.'

'And the other reason?'

'Well, the other reason is that I don't intend to end up stretchin' a rope. I don't worry much about gettin' shot, should some fella be faster'n me. I do worry some about gettin' hung. I seen fellas hung, and that ain't no way to die. That's why I don't never

call anybody out when I'm clear out away from everything, if I can help it. I want folks around. I want
honest folks around, not just guys that work for the
other side. I want folks to be able to say I gave the
other guy a fair shake, that I let 'im go fer his gun
either afore I did, er at least at the same time. I ain't
never been in trouble with the law, and I don't aim ta
be.'

'So your idea of how to help us is to just keep finding the ranchers' gunfighters alone, or maybe two or
three together, and challenge them to draw, so you
can kill them.'

He pursed his lips and thought a moment. 'I 'spect
that about covers it. Sooner er later they'll run outa
hired guns, er the ones they got'll spook an' quit the
country 'cause they know I killed faster men than
them. Then the ranchers'll back down.'

'And if they don't, then what? Will you start doing
the same thing to the ranchers?'

He thought about that idea for a long moment
before he answered. 'I s'pose, if it comes ta that, but
that'd bother me some. The ranchers ain't innocent
by any stretch o' the imagination. They're the ones
hirin' all the gun hands ta kill your herders an' run
'em off. An' me too, if they can. But they got families.
They got wives an' kids. The women an' kids didn't
hire no gunmen or try to run off the sheep-ranchers,
so they don't deserve to lose their men. Like I say, if
it comes ta that, I suppose I'll have to, but not up to
then.'

'Do you know what I think?'

'Nope. Prob'ly just as well, too.'

50

Ignoring the barb, she said: 'I think you're not nearly as hard and callous as you think you are.'

He hoped she was wrong. He knew that if she wasn't, sooner or later he'd hesitate, maybe just for part of a second. Part of a second would be too much.

Her mouth opened and closed again. She shook her head. 'I don't know what's coming over me. Here I stand, talking about killing people as if we're discussing the weather. And being glad, and proud that . . . it's . . . this . . . I am becoming. . . .'

'It's a hard country,' Flint observed.

She looked back and forth between Amado and Flint several times. Then she spoke. 'Yes, it is. And so is the truth. We cannot do this, can we, Mr Tucker?'

'Flint.'

'Mr Flint,' she corrected. 'We cannot win.'

'What'dya mean?'

'I mean we cannot win. We're lying to ourselves. We're trying to teach men to shoot who have never touched a gun in their lives. They're coming here from all the other sheep ranches, so you can teach them to shoot.'

'They're learnin',' he defended.

'Of course they are. But not well enough. Not fast enough. Not enough of them. We don't even have guns enough. We have nearly fifty men, and no more than ten rifles. Even if all of them learned to shoot well, we don't have the guns to give them, and that's what we promised.'

'We did keep the rifles o' the three today.' Even to Flint it sounded lame.

51

She actually snorted through her nose. 'Oh, that makes it better. Now we have thirteen rifles, for fifty men to share.'

'You didn't figger that out afore ya hired me?'

She waved her empty hand in frustration. 'I don't know. Yes. No. I don't know. It just sounded like our last . . . it sounded like the only chance we had, to hire someone who knew about . . . I wanted the ranchers to know we're serious. That we're not leaving. That they'll have to kill us to get rid of us, and we won't die easily. That's what I wanted. I didn't want it to come to this.'

'You thought they wouldn't really fight?'

She whirled to face him squarely. 'Yes! That's exactly what I thought! I thought if we showed enough fight, they'd back off.'

Flint scowled at her. 'They'll back off when they know they gotta. Not before. The only way we can force that is to get enough of your herders good enough to defend their outfits.'

She shook her head. 'Aren't you listening to me? It's not enough. We don't have time. We don't have enough people. We don't have enough guns even if they learn to shoot. And when the other sheep get here it will all come to a head. . . .'

Flint jerked a hand up and grabbed the arm with which she was gesturing. 'What? What other sheep? What are you talking about?'

She jerked her arm out of his grip and glared at him. 'The rest of the sheep. That's the other part of our wonderful plan that's just going to get us all killed.'

Flint's voice went flat. He spoke softly, but the words broke from his mouth like brittle steel. 'Maybe you'd best tell me the whole story. Now.'

She glared hotly at him for half a minute, then her eyes melted, brimming with tears. She lifted her free hand and let it drop to her side. 'It sounded like a good plan. We all agreed on it. We would hire you, and you would teach us how to defend our land and our livestock. At the same time we sent for enough sheep to bolster the numbers of our herds. That's why none of the sheepmen has any cash now. There are six thousand more sheep bought, between the six of us. We each bought another thousand sheep. They're being shipped on the railroad. They'll be at the railhead in another two weeks. We thought the extra numbers and having you here would convince the cattlemen we were here to stay, and they'd leave us alone.'

Flint swore softly, fiercely. 'Anything else you ain't bothered to tell me?'

She shook her head. Her voice was resigned. 'No. That's all. That's enough. It was a stupid idea to begin with. The cattlemen are just hiring more and more gunfighters instead. When the rest of the sheep get here, they'll know they have to move. Then they'll come. They'll come with their hired gunfighters, and all we'll have is a bunch of Mexicans with knives and ten rifles. Oh, excuse me. Thirteen rifles. However many. Not nearly enough. And we will all die. And the cattlemen and their hired gunmen will kill and scatter our sheep and let the wolves have them, and they will have the whole country to themselves. And we won't even care, because we will all be dead.'

Flint scoured his mind for something to answer. There was nothing there to offer. In his heart of hearts, he knew she was exactly right.

CHAPTER 7

'Amado will stick around the place today.'

Betty glowered at him. 'Mr Tucker, I do not need a nursemaid. I am perfectly capable of taking care of myself.'

Flint's expression did not change. 'No offense, ma'am, but that ain't so. Fact is, Amado ain't no match for the likes o' them the ranchers been bringin' inta the country, let alone you.'

A flicker of recognition flashed briefly in her eyes. 'Is that why Ian and the others decided you needed to make my ranch the place where you stayed.'

His nod was reluctant, but affirmative. 'The others got menfolk. They ain't no match for the ranchers' gunmen neither, but they'll give 'em pause at least. You ain't got nobody 'cept your herders. They're likely ta do things ta you what folks don't talk about, just ta scare the others off.'

Anger suffused her face briefly, then the import of his words penetrated her umbrage and the color fled from her face, leaving her momentarily pale and wide-eyed. Unconsciously she lifted the rifle she held loosely in her left hand, and gripped it with the right as well. Her eyes darted involuntarily around the tops of the hills surrounding the ranch buildings.

She collected herself with obvious effort. 'You're not going to be teaching herders to use the rifles today?'

'Nope. Feelin' too much like a danged school-teacher. Last bunch is as good as they're gonna get for now. Five new ones comin' in day after tomorrow, so I'll have ta start over. At least I'm gettin' the speech I start with down pat.'

'Are they learning well?'

He nodded. 'Fair ta middlin'. Better'n that, I guess. Some of 'em are gettin' good already.'

'What are you going to do today?'

'Headin' inta town.'

'If you're going for supplies, I could stand to go too.'

His hesitation lasted only an instant. 'Sooner ya didn't.'

Her eyes searched his. 'Why not? If you don't mind my asking, that is.'

'I do.'

'Do what?'

'Mind.'

With that he wheeled and left her sputtering in the middle of the yard. She was still standing there when he rode out of the barn and left the yard at a swift trot. Her eyes darted about wildly until she spotted Amado. He was standing in the shadow of the bunkhouse, where he had a clear view of the yard and all the buildings. One of the Winchester 73s rested in the crook of his arm.

Her eyes darted around the rim of hills again. She turned and went into the house. She set her own rifle carefully by the door, then hurried to shut and bar the back door, which would be out of Amado's line of sight. A tiny shudder ran through her body as she realized how suddenly alone and vulnerable she felt with Flint gone.

Flint sat at the head of Main Street, sizing up the town. He made mental note of the number of horses tied up outside the saLoon, and how many of the saddles showed evidence that they belonged to working cowboys, and how many had no scars from ropes, angry horns, and scratching brush. 'Five gun hands, six cowpokes,' he told his horse softly. The horse's only response was to shake his head, then lower it to scratch the side of his mouth on the inside of a front leg.

He sat there thinking, his face its usual impassive mask. A smile abruptly broke the dour sameness of his expression, before it quickly vanished and his mouth returned to the non-commital line across his face. He lifted the reins and nudged his horse forward.

Half an hour later he emerged from Steinberg's Mercantile Store with a gallon can of kerosene. He walked back between the store and the building next to it, then walked another block, keeping parallel with one of the town's two streets, on a line well behind the houses that faced that street. At the cowshed behind one of the houses, he glanced around carefully, then ducked into the shed. As he had hoped, the family's milk-cow was in a stall, contentedly munching hay. He set the can of kerosene down and picked up a flat pan, obviously used to put out milk for the family cats.

He stepped into the stall, crooning softly to ease the animal's discomfort at the presence of a stranger. When she stopped fidgeting around the stall, he knelt and quickly began to milk her into the flat pan. When it was nearly full, he stepped quickly from the stall.

He picked up the kerosene with one hand and looked around the shed. He set both burdens on the earth floor of the shed and stepped to a piece of old flour-sack hanging from the side of an empty stall. He tore an inch-wide strip from it, stuffed it into his pocket, then replaced the rest of the rag.

Picking up both the pan of milk and the kerosene, he stuck his head out the door and looked in all directions he could see. He stepped out quickly, retracing his steps to the back of the mercantile store.

Instead of going on out to the street, he followed the back of the businesses down the street to the livery barn. There he set the kerosene and pan of milk on the ground, backed up to the side of the building and squatted down with his back to the wall. He fished the bag of tobacco from his pocket, rolled a cigarette and lit it. He stayed there until he had finished the smoke.

As he ground it out beneath his heel he looked carefully around. He spotted four cats, drawn by the smell of the warm milk, but staying almost hidden.

He squatted by the pan. 'Here kitty, kitty,' he said softly.

The second time he called, one of the cats moved out of its partial concealment and started forward. As if that were a signal, the four he had spotted and two he had not raced forward to partake of the proffered treat. He reached down and touched one, to stroke its back. It yowled and leaped away from him, then returned to the pan of milk from the opposite side, lapping feverishly.

He tried another. It arched its back slightly to his touch and began to purr almost at once.

He continued to pet and scratch the cat until the pan was licked dry. As the others looked at him as if to ask if there was more, he stood, lifting the amiable cat with him. He stepped into the shelter of the livery barn.

Holding the cat with one hand, he poured kerosene onto the strip of rag he had removed from his pocket. When it was thoroughly soused with the substance, he wrapped one end of it around the cat's tail, close to the body, and tied it snugly. The cat began to squirm.

Crooning softly to the cat, scratching its ears with the hand that held it, he wrapped the kerosene-soaked rag around and around its tail. At the end of the tail he again tied it in a knot, holding it firmly in place.

He stepped to the front of the livery barn and looked up and down the street. Three people were on the sidewalk, walking leisurely. He waited until they had all disappeared into one building or another, then walked quickly across to the saLoon. He moved as silently as he could along the wall until he was right beside the door.

He listened for a minute to the sounds that carried out past the batwing-doors. He squatted down, took a match from his pocket, and struck it on the back of his pants leg. The cat was squirming more and more. He touched the match to the end of the kerosene-saturated rag and watched the flame swiftly envelope the hapless animal's tail.

As the cat stiffened it emitted a piercing yowl. He tossed it beneath the batwing-doors as far into the saLoon as he could, then retreated to the center of the street, selecting a spot that could not be seen from the saloon's interior.

Bedlam erupted in Bub's saloon. The frantic and agonized yowling of the cat was followed by yells, wild curses, chairs and tables flying, and glasses and bottles breaking. One strident voice boomed above the others, yelling: 'Slap them fires out or the whole place'll go up!'

Even above the bedlam he could hear jackets and chaps slapping down flames that had sprung up in the sawdust that covered the floor.

Just then the cat shot out of the door, finding at last an avenue to freedom and daylight. The kerosene had burnt itself out, leaving a hairless, charred rope of a tail still smoldering. The cat continued its piercing yowl as it streaked across the street and disappeared between two buildings.

Up and down the street people began to poke their heads out of doors and windows to find out the

source of the racket. When they spotted Flint standing in the middle of the street, most of them ducked
back inside just as quickly.

Less than three minutes passed before the bedlam
began to quieten and men came stumbling out
through the door, coughing and rubbing their eyes
from the smoke.

As those in the lead spotted Flint they stopped so
abruptly they were nearly bowled to the ground by
those behind them. In the flurry of questions, curses
and coughs, he heard his name mentioned several
times.

A small, lean man with an expression at least as
hard as Flint's stepped through the cluster of men
out into the street, watching Flint carefully. The tall-
crowned hat he wore looked comically large on him.
Its effect was to make him appear even smaller than
he was. His hand hovered just above the grip of a .36
caliber Colt revolver.

Two others followed him, spacing themselves
about three feet from the first one. They looked so
much alike they might have been twins. Their faces
bore the same features, even to the detail of having
moustaches trimmed precisely alike. Each wore a
tied-down Colt .45 on each hip. They wore flat-
crowned hats that announced they were from the
South-west. 'Arizona Territory', Flint mentally
commented.

One of the twins spoke. 'You the ring-tailed
bastard that pulled that stunt?'

'Nope,' Flint said, forcing his voice to be calm and
amiable. 'I ain't ring-tailed, and I do know who my

61

dad was. I 'spect that's hard for folks that never had one to understand, though. I am the gentleman who provided you boys that little bit o' diversion an' recreation. You ain't gonna take exception to that, now, are you?'

'Are you the one they call Flint?' the small man asked softly.

'That's what folks call me.'

'I was hoping to meet you. The sooner the better.'

He was fast. Probably the fastest Flint had ever seen. Certainly the fastest he had faced. His finely honed instincts told him the man would draw as soon as that word was said. It was only that instinct which allowed him to draw and fire the barest instant ahead of the little man's .36. The impact of the .44 cartridge from Flint's Russian drove him backward. His effort to resist the force of the bullet's blow caused him to twist sideways, even as his well-conditioned reflex concluded his draw by squeezing the trigger. The gun, however, was no longer pointed at Flint. Instead his bullet buried itself in the stomach of a man in the group of cowboys clustered at the door of Bub's saloon.

Even before the little man's gun fired, Flint's Russian .44 had spit a piece of hot lead into the heart of one of the twins, even as it continued its path to line up with the second and fire again. The three shots from Flint's revolver were so closely spaced they sounded almost as if it were one elongated report.

The first of the twins did not yet have his gun out of the holster when Flint's bullet stopped his intention. The second twin's gun barrel was just clearing leather when the life was driven from him by Flint's third shot.

Without wasting a glance at any of the three, Flint swung the gun to cover the cluster of cowboys who gaped at the carnage in the street. Almost nonchalantly he slid the Colt Peacemaker out of its holster, so that he had two guns with which to intimidate them. 'Anyone else wanta take exception to a friendly joke?'

Nobody offered to do so.

'Then I'll give you a bit of advice. No matter what they tell ya, the ranchers can't bring in enough gunfighters ta keep you boys from gettin' yourselves killed along with 'em, if you don't back off an' leave the sheep-ranchers alone. You boys better talk some sense into their heads, or else pack up your stuff and find friendlier country to punch cows in. An' tell whatever o' them gun hands you happen ta talk to, that they ain't gettin' paid near enough ta have ta face the likes o' me.'

He waited just a minute for his words to sink in. 'Now you boys best get back inside afore I start gettin' nervous.'

With less than a second of hesitation, those closest to Flint started crowding back, forcing the others to retreat into the dim interior. When the last of them were back inside, Flint turned and strode swiftly to the livery barn. Mounting his horse he rode out the back door of the edifice, trotted swiftly down a side street to the edge of town, then followed around in a wide circle to regain the trail back to the Burton ranch.

The sun was just settling behind the mountains to the west when he trotted into the yard. He hadn't reached the barn when Betty stepped out of the house. 'It's all right, Amado,' she called. 'It's Flint.'

Amado stepped out of the shadows by the corral, still cradling his rifle. '*Sí*, Señora. I have my sights on him until I recognize him. I go eat supper now.'

'Did you have any trouble in town?'

'No more'n I could handle.'

'Then you had trouble?'

He looked at her a long moment. Then he said: 'They got three less gun hands. I'd call that maybe savin' a bit o' trouble down the line.'

Her soft gasp did not escape his attention. 'You killed three more of their gunfighters?'

'Yes ma'am. That an' put an awful hurt on a cat's tail.'

He almost laughed at the confusion written on her face. When she didn't stop staring at him with that inquisitive, demanding look, he told her at last what he had done.

'Oh, Flint! That's terrible! Oh, that poor cat! However could you do such a thing?'

He smiled in spite of himself. 'You're gettin' into this range war thing way too much. I killed three men today, an' all you feel anythin' for is a cat with a burnt tail?'

She opened her mouth and closed it again. Even in the dim interior of the barn he could see her face redden. For just a moment he thought how beautiful she was. He quickly suppressed the thought and strode from the barn.

He was nearly to the cook shack to find something to eat when she called to him. 'Oh, Flint?'

He stopped and turned. 'Yes, ma'am?'

'You said the next herders won't be here for you to teach them to shoot until day after tomorrow. Would you have some free time tomorrow?'

'For what, ma'am?'

'I . . . that is . . . I really need to collect some wild onions, some wild rhubarb, and quite a few other herbs and things. There's a place about five miles up, along the creek at the edge of the timber, which has almost everything I need. I was going to do that tomorrow, then I thought about it and . . . and . . . and about what you said earlier, and . . . well, I'm . . . that is, do you think it would be safe for me to do that?'

There was no hesitation. 'No, ma'am.'

She, on the other hand, hesitated a long moment. 'Would . . . could I ask you to accompany me, then?'

A feeling he could never remember surged up in him, stifled at once, but powerful none the less. He took a breath before answering. 'I guess I didn't have no better plans.'

'Oh, good,' she responded. 'We'll leave just after breakfast.'

CHAPTER 8

'Get up that tree! That's a grizzly sow.'

'What? Where?'

'Comin' up towards us, right down there.'

Betty looked down the line of Flint's pointing finger. She could barely see the hump on the back of a bear, showing briefly from time to time.

'She won't bother us, will she? We're not bothering her.'

'She's a grizzly. They ain't no tellin' what a grizzly'll do. 'Specially this early in the summer. She's likely got a cub. Sometimes they'll run from you. Sometimes they'll hunt you, just to see if'n they kin kill ya. Anyway, I ain't takin' no chances. Get up that tree.'

Betty looked at the bulbs she had dug, which she was holding in her apron. She looked up at the lowest branch of the tree Flint was frantically indicating. She lifted her chin. 'I'm not a child! And I am not going to show my legs like some brazen hussy trying to climb a tree I'm much too old to climb, just because you think—'

Flint cut her off. 'She's smelled us! Get up there! Fast!'

Betty looked back at where she had last seen the bear. She saw the bear's snout lifted above the bushes, sampling the air. Just then the bear emitted an angry growl. She stood on her hind legs to see over the brush, and spotted them immediately.

'Oh, dear!' Betty cried.

She dropped the bulbs from her apron and began scrambling to get into the tree. She grabbed the lowest branch, but she couldn't quite hoist herself to it. Throwing modesty to the winds, Flint stepped forward and grabbed her. He hoisted her as far as he could. She grasped the branch and held herself momentarily. Flint put both hands on her rear and heaved with all his might. Betty managed to get onto the branch.

'Now climb higher!' Flint roared at her. 'She can reach you there, but she can't climb. Now move!'

The limbs were now in close proximity, so Betty began to climb the branches like rungs of a ladder. Flint sprinted to his horse. As he leaped into the saddle he saw the bear approaching the tree. The grizzly's lumbering gait made her look slow, but she covered the intervening ground with amazing speed. Betty was watching her too. With a stifled squeal she realized how quickly the bear was approaching, and redoubled her efforts to climb through the thick branches of the northern pine-tree.

The bear reached the tree and lunged at its trunk. It stretched upwards as far as it could reach, barely missing Betty's foot. The claw brushed by her shoe and struck the tree, snapped off several branches like toothpicks, then dragged down the trunk, leaving rows of claw marks dug into the soft wood.

Roaring frustration and mindless rage, the bear grasped the tree with its front paws and began to shake it. In spite of the fact that the tree was large, the force of the furious animal began to make it quiver and sway. Betty screamed in fear. 'Flint! Do something! She's going to shake me out of here!'

Flint was already in action. He levered a shell into his Winchester 73 carbine, already painfully aware of its inadequacy. The blunt slug of the rifle would only infuriate the bear, he knew. The chance of a kill with a single shot was almost non-existent with a bear of that size. If he could hit it in the eye, or in the open mouth, it was possible, but not otherwise. The shell would penetrate the bear's hide, but not with sufficient velocity or force to exact a swift kill. The bear would die, but only after several hours.

He knew, however, that if the bear was left to shake the tree, it might succeed in dislodging Betty. If she fell from the tree, nothing he could do would keep the bear from killing her.

Just then the terror-stricken team jerked loose from their tethers and galloped away, taking with them the wagon Betty had driven there. The commotion scarcely distracted the bear from the smell of the frightened, screaming woman in the tree.

Flint clamped his spurs to his horse. In spite of its own fear, the horse responded bravely. Riding at a dead run, Flint raced past the bear, yelling at the top of his voice. As he passed by, he fired his rifle into the tree trunk, right in front of the bear. A shower of bark and splinters flew into her face.

With a roar of surprise and rage she wheeled from the tree and lashed out at the horse and rider. They were moving fast enough to be barely out of reach by the time she whirled, but she immediately set out in pursuit.

The brush was too thick for the horse to run any distance. It whipped at the horse's body, lashing at Flint's legs and face. The smell and sound of the angry bear instilled an immense surge of strength in the horse, however, and he lunged through the obstacles, keeping his distance from the bear.

When they were less than a hundred yards from the tree, the bear stopped. The breeze had carried scent of the woman to it again. It remembered the source of its original anger. It turned and began to lumber back toward the tree.

Flint wheeled his frightened horse and raced back toward the animal. He levered another shell into his rifle. Passing as close as he thought he dared, he again yelled at the top of his lungs. He fired the rifle into the ground, kicking up dirt and debris from a foot in front of the bear's nose.

With incredible speed the bear whirled, lashing out with a forepaw. The blow was so close she came away with a clump of hair from the tail of Flint's mount. The terrified animal squealed in fear and lunged through the brush. The bear followed in hot pursuit.

The fear that propelled the horse allowed him to open up a sizeable lead over the pursuing bear. Then his front hoof snagged a hidden branch in the thick vegetation. His feet were jerked out from under him.

Flint shot over his head. He landed in the brush with a crash that shook every bone in his body. His rifle arced away to land somewhere out of sight.

The horse, squealing in terror, lunged to his feet. He ran, reins streaming, from the source of his panic.

Flint scrambled to his feet. He lunged after his retreating mount. The crashing of the pursuing bear in the brush grew swiftly closer. As he ran he unfastened the strap that held his Peacemaker revolver in its holster. He looked over his shoulder. With sickening realization, he saw that the bear would be upon him in seconds.

He ran as fast as he could in the impeding brush. He waited until the bear was as close as he could tolerate. He whirled and fired two quick shots into the ground, right in front of her. The unexpected turn, the noise and flash, the smell of burned gunpowder, and the shower of dirt and debris momentarily shocked the bear. She set her legs in rigid bracing, and skidded to a stop.

Flint took advantage of the break to look for a tree to climb. There was none that would hold him, that he could hope to reach in time. He began to run. The bear roared her renewed fury and set out in pursuit again.

Then Flint spotted his horse. One of the trailing reins, flying beside him, had whipped around the trunk of a sapling and formed a half-hitch, securing the rein to the tree. The horse was braced against it, pulling for all he was worth. His ears were flattened back against his head. His eyes rolled in mindless terror. His breath came in squeals of fear.

Flint lunged for him. Just as he almost reached him, the tangled rein broke free. The sudden release of the tether almost caused the bay gelding to fall backward. He recovered immediately and lunged into an all-out run.

The near fall was the only thing that allowed Flint to reach him. As he recovered and whirled to flee, Flint gave a desperate leap. He caught the saddle horn. His foot hit the ground once as he gave the best kick he was able. The momentum of the lunging horse carried him airborne. He gripped the saddle horn in grim determination. He pulled himself into the saddle.

Just as he hit the saddle a low branch swatted him in the head. His hat flew off. Blackness threatened to engulf him. He shook his head and pulled himself down over the saddle horn. His right foot managed to find the flying stirrup. He slid his boot into it. He leaned forward, reaching for the flying reins. He managed to catch first one, then the other. Just then the horse broke clear of the brush and trees. His speed increased. The grass and sagebrush became a blur beneath his thundering hoofs. Flint settled more securely into the saddle. His vision cleared. He began to talk to his horse, and to haul on the reins.

It took fully 400 yards for Flint to begin exerting any control whatever on the panicked animal. By degrees its panic gave way to its training, and he began to respond. As soon as he could, Flint looked over his shoulder to find the bear.

She had emerged from the brush along the creek

and stood in the open. When they hit the open ground, which allowed the horse to run, she quickly realized she could not catch them and stopped. She stood, head lowered, swinging it back and forth from side to side. She continually emitted a rumbling growl of frustrated anger.

Flint swung his horse around. Although reluctant to do anything except put space between himself and the bear, the animal obeyed. Flint galloped to within fifty yards of the bear and turned his horse sideways. He yelled: 'C'mon ya stupid sow! Here I am! Come an' git me!'

The bear responded by roaring her anger. She stood on her hind legs, reaching out her forelegs like a boxer, flailing the air in front of her. Then she dropped to all fours again to come lumbering after them. She quickly stopped again, however, when horse and rider galloped away.

Now how'm I gonna get her far enough away without gettin' too close fer comfort? Flint wondered.

His horse's actions made it abundantly clear that *his* comfort barrier had already been crossed. Just then a bear-cub broke into the clear from the bushes, 200 yards from the old sow. The old she-bear responded at once, changing courses and loping toward it.

Mother and cub spent a brief moment in reunion, then the bear shambled back into the bushes, moving directly away from the tree in which Betty remained. She neither looked at the tormenting horseman, nor gave any indication she had ever been aware of his existence.

Flint let out a long sigh of relief. 'Now ain't that somethin'?' he marveled. 'Just like that, she ambles off an' pretends she ain't never been mad at nobody in 'er whole life.'

He retraced his course through the trampled brush. He marveled at the path of destruction the three of them had wrought. He retrieved his hat and examined it. 'Well, at least she didn't tear it up none.' He grinned.

It took a while longer to find his rifle. When he did, he examined it carefully. He checked to be sure nothing had become lodged in the barrel. He levered the action to be sure a fresh shell was in the chamber. He replaced the spent cartridges in the magazine. He took time then to talk to his horse, and to pet away the last vestiges of his fright. The animal steadied down readily under his hand and voice. He started tearing grass from beside a nearby bush and munching it.

Flint rode back toward Betty, listening intently for any indication that the bear had again reversed her direction or changed her mind.

'Flint? Is that you?'

'Yup,' he called back. 'She's gone. I got 'er off fur enough she found 'er cub an' forgot about you.'

'Oh, thank God,' Betty breathed. 'I don't know if I could have stayed up in this tree another minute.'

Flint looked around. 'I 'spect it'd be a good idea if 'n you did,' he suggested. 'She might come back, an' it'll take me a while to chase down that team. It'd be best if 'n you could get as comfortable as you can up there, an' just stay put till I get back with 'em.'

He didn't wait to hear her protests. He set out in search of the team that had bolted with the wagon.

His mind was already forming an image of helping her down from the tree, when he returned. He could almost feel her slender waist inside the circle of his arm. He remembered suddenly the feel of her backside against his hands as he hoisted her into the tree.

He knew he needed to stifle those thoughts instantly. It was exactly those kinds of emotions that would make a man careless, divert his mind, get him killed. But the thoughts felt so good! They evoked feelings he had thought long dead within him. He reveled in them, even as he found and caught the frightened team.

He had no way to know about the similar thoughts that roiled through Betty's mind as she sat in the tree awaiting his return.

CHAPTER 9

'Señor Flint. There is a rider coming. Andres, who is on the hill, has signaled that it is one man riding alone.'

'Any idea who?'

'No, *señor*.'

'Well, shouldn't be a problem. Thanks, Amado.'

'*Sí, señor.* I will watch from the corral.'

Flint nodded absently. He wondered fleetingly if his tactic of picking off the rancher's best gunfighters was going to result in some kind of peace overture. He shrugged.

He walked to the house and knocked on the door. Betty answered, almost immediately. Alarm vibrated through her voice. 'What is it?'

'Nothin' to be concerned about, I 'spect. Andres on the hill signaled a lone rider comin' in. Just thought you'd like to know.'

'I'll see who it is. It might be one of the neighbors.'

'Could be.'

Flint idled near the barn door where he could watch the trail that approached the ranch. It was less

75

than five minutes before he could see the rider. Before he could make out any other feature, he caught the sun's brilliant reflection from the rider's chest.

He called to Betty, sitting in a rocking-chair on the porch of the house. 'Sportin' a badge. Seems to be a lawman.'

'How can you tell from this distance?'

'Sun shinin' off something on his shirt. Most likely a badge. Who's the law around here?'

'There isn't any this side of Buffalo. There's a sheriff there, but I've never seen him out here.'

'Any US Marshals around?'

'Not that I've heard of. There's not a lot of law in this country yet. That's why the cattlemen have had free rein.'

Flint stepped back inside the barn, watching from the dimmer interior as the rider entered the yard. The star on his chest was prominently displayed. It was not surrounded by the circle that indicated a US Marshal. 'Must be the sheriff,' he muttered.

He waited while the rider approached the porch where Betty stood to greet him. 'Get down and come in,' she invited. 'Coffee-pot's always on.'

The lawman did not dismount. 'Mrs Burton?'

'That's me.'

'Sheriff Regan.'

'You're a long way from Buffalo.'

'My duty says I have to police the whole county. You got a fella workin' for you by the name of Flint?'

'Why? Is he wanted for something?'

'Can't say. I'd be obliged to have a word with him.'

'Did I hear my name?' Flint asked, approaching the sheriff from the rear.

The sheriff stiffened and reined his horse around, backing him several steps, so he could see Flint and Betty at the same time. 'You Tucker?'

Flint nodded. 'Most folks call me Flint.'

'Where you from, Tucker?'

'Oh, here an' there. Never lived in one spot long enough to be from it, I guess.'

The sheriff frowned. 'What are you doing here?'

'Working for Mrs Burton. There anything wrong with that?'

The sheriff's eyes narrowed. 'Don't play word games with me, Tucker. You're a gunman.'

'I sorta noticed a heavy population o' them in this county, Sheriff. That somethin' you approve, the ranchers importin' 'em in them numbers?'

The sheriff ignored the question. 'I've received reports of you deliberately starting confrontations and deliberately murdering several men.'

Flint shook his head. His voice lowered and flattened. 'Murder's a pretty loaded word, Sheriff. I've never murdered a man in my life. There have been several lately that've confronted me, with the clear intention of killing me. If you'll ask around, you'll find plenty o' witnesses to tell you every one of 'em started the festivities themselves. I didn't. I just defended myself.'

'Self-defense don't give a man a right to set people up to be killed.'

Flint shrugged. 'I didn't start anything with anyone. I never challenged anyone. I never made any suggestion that anyone go for his gun. Like I said, there were a whole lot o' witnesses. If you ask anyone that don't hang out in Bub's place, you'll find I'm tellin' the truth.'

'Tucker, I'm the law in this county. I think you're a threat to the peace and well-being of the area. I'm ordering you out of the county.'

'Well, now, that's something I don't guess you got any right to do.'

'I'm the law in this county!'

'No, I don't guess that's so,' Flint countered. 'You're the sheriff. The sheriff is sworn to uphold the law, if I'm not mistaken. That's a whole world o' difference from bein' the law. You got no more right to go beyond the law than I do. I don't think there's any reason within the law that'd let you order me outa the county.'

The sheriff's face reddened as his eyes narrowed. 'There ain't room in this county for hired gunfighters.'

'Did you tell that to the ranchers?'

'I ain't here to talk about the ranchers. I'm here to talk about you.'

'You already did that. Now let's talk about the ranchers. By my last count, they got more than twenty hired gunfighters on their payroll, an' more ridin' in 'most every day. It looks ta me like you got the makin's of a full-blown range war on your hands, Sheriff. If you're aimin' ta head it off, I 'spect the place ta start would be with the ones hirin' the most gunhands.'

'I don't need you tellin' me how to do my job.'

'You sure o' that? Seems ta me you're goin' about

it plumb backward. Have you told any o' them ranchers ta git rid o' their gunfighters? 'Cause if you ain't, it'd sure look like you're more interested in doin' the biddin' o' the ranchers than doin' your job an' upholdin' the law.'

'I can come back here with a posse and take you down a peg, Tucker.'

'Maybe. But if you come onto this land with a bunch o' gunfighters, we'll have to assume you're just a patsy for the ranchers an' treat you like we would any other outlaw. We got a right to defend ourselves.'

'I'll have a warrant sworn out for your arrest.'

'On what charge?'

'Murder.'

'Who'd I murder?'

'Whip Henshaw, for one.'

'He drew first. That's self-defense.'

'So you say.'

'Like I said, there were plenty o' witnesses.'

'I've a mind to arrest you right here and now.'

Flint almost smiled. 'If you think you can, I guess you can try. If you ain't got a warrant or anything more'n the cooked-up charges you been bandyin' about, I'd think twice about it, if I was you.'

'Are you threatening a sworn officer of the law?'

'I wouldn't dream o' doin' such a thing. I think that'd be against the law. I'm just offerin' a friendly bit of advice. You married, Sheriff?'

Caught off guard by the question, a long silence hung ahead of his answer. 'What's that got to do with anything?'

'Just wonderin'.'

'As a matter of fact I am. Why would that be any of your business?'

Flint shrugged. 'It ain't really. I was just thinkin'. I 'spect your wife's hopin' you make it back ta Buffalo.'

Another silence as the sheriff frowned. 'What's that supposed to mean.'

'That means you best not try ta arrest me without a reason. That means afore ya start throwin' the weight o' your office around at the sheep-ranchers, ya best line up whatever help ya need to make the cattlemen pull in their horns. You're sorta in a tough spot, Sheriff. You can't arrest me or run me outa the country. I don't run, an' I don't think you're good enough to take me in. You can't make the cattlemen pull in their horns, 'cause they got a whole passel o' gunmen that'd love a chance ta do ya in. You're sorta stuck out in the middle, here, Sheriff.'

'Since you seem to be an expert, just what do you propose I do about that?'

Flint shrugged again. 'Just sorta feelin' glad I ain't the sheriff. But since ya asked, I 'spect the best thing to do'd be ta ask the army ta step in. They got the manpower. The fort ain't that far off. They can enforce the law on the cattlemen just as well as the sheepmen. They can stop this thing blowin' up into a range war. I doubt anything else can, since it's already gone this far.'

'I don't need the army to tell me how to do my job.'

'Suit yourself. Just make sure you ain't on the wrong side when the dust settles.'

The sheriff acted as if he was going to bluster further, but then reined his horse around and rode out of the yard at a lope. They watched in silence as he shrunk into the distance and disappeared. Amado came out of the shadows to stand beside Flint as they watched. 'Can he do any of that?' Betty asked at last.

Flint shook his head slowly. 'I ain't sure there's a thing in the world he can do. If he tries to run me outa the country, I'll kill 'im. If he tries to make the cattlemen get rid o' their hired guns, they'll kill 'im. If I was him, I think I'd be real busy in Buffalo till this thing's all over.'

'Could he call in the army?'

'Sure he could, if he wanted to. But the cattlemen put him in office. The army'd put a stop ta their plans ta get rid of all the sheepmen. I don't s'pose he dares do that either.'

'Then there won't be any help from him or the army, either one?'

'Nope. We're on our own.'

Those words echoed a lot more ominously than he had planned.

CHAPTER 10

He was running as fast as his legs would carry him. He waved his arms frantically above his head. His serape flowed out behind him. As if they had eyes of their own, his feet dodged around rocks, leaped over low scrubs of sage, and evaded holes in the ground without slackening his speed.

The two riders squinted at the frantic man, small in the distance.

'That is Renaldo, Señor Flint,' Amado observed.

'Seems to be plumb excited about somethin'.'

'*Sí.*'

'Let's see what the problem is.'

Flint jammed his spurs into his horse's side at the same time as he leaned forward and yelled: 'Hyeaah!'

The horse responded as if shot from a cannon. He leaped forward, reaching full stride in four jumps. Flint felt the front brim of his hat fold up tightly against the crown. The wind irritated his eyes, making him squint. He could hear Amado's horse laboring to keep up.

As soon as they began to run toward him, Renaldo stopped, waiting. He was still huffing and puffing as

Flint skidded his horse to a halt beside the herder.

'What's wrong, Renaldo?'

'It is the wolves have come, *señor*! The wolves have come! The wolves are in my sheeps, and I cannot stop them. I do not have the gun. They have kill my dog. *Por favor*, Señor Flint, you must save my sheeps.'

'Where's your flock?'

He turned and pointed, bouncing up and down in agitation. 'They are just over that hill, *señor*. I see them coming into the sheeps. My dog, he sees them, and he tries to protect the sheeps like Renaldo does. The wolves, they kill him. I see you coming in the distance here, and I can do nothing but come as fast as my legs will come with me. I can shoot now, because you teach me, but I do not have the gun to shoot when I am with my sheeps.'

Flint frowned. 'Well, I guess there's no hurry. They've likely already killed a sheep or two, and they'll be busy eatin'.'

Renaldo bounced up and down even faster. 'No, no, *señor*! That is why I run to make you hurry so fast as ever you can do, *señor*. They are not coyotes, *señor*. They are wolves. They are killing my sheeps! Hurry, Señor Flint! They are killing and killing!'

Flint looked at Amado in confusion. Instead of answering, Amado wheeled his horse the way Renaldo had pointed and spurred the animal to a dead run. Still confused, Flint followed.

His horse decided it was a race and rose to the challenge. He stretched out his stride until his belly brushed the tallest of the grass with every stride. The ground around them turned to a blur as Flint fought to keep his eyes from watering and blurring his vision as well. By the time they reached the top of the hill over which Renaldo had run, he had nearly caught up with Amado.

Amado hesitated only an instant at the crest of the hill, then spurred his horse forward. Letting his own mount maintain his effort to catch the other, Flint stood in his stirrups to see what lay before him.

The hill sloped down and leveled off into a broad, shallow valley. In one end of the valley was a large pond, either fed by some hidden spring or by trapped rainwater. The valley teemed with a flock of nearly 1,400 sheep.

Directly in front of them, in the lowest part of the valley, bedlam reigned within the herd. Sheep were running this way and that, bleating in terror, running into each other, changing direction to run into other of their fellows. When one would break into the open for a brief moment, he would almost immediately whirl and run back into the bunch, incapable of running any place except toward other sheep.

In the middle of the vast expanse of sheep four large wolves were wreaking havoc. Crazed with blood and easy victims, they were pouncing on sheep and ripping their throats out. As quickly as blood gushed from a throat, that wolf would wheel and spring on a different sheep.

When he decided he was close enough, Amado sprang from his horse. Dropping to one knee to steady himself, exactly as Flint had taught him, he aimed at one of the wolves and fired.

The wolf yelped in pain and surprise. It whirled to

snap at the cause of the sudden pain, but there was nothing there. Then it toppled sideways.

Amado was ecstatic. 'I did it, Señor Flint! I did it! I did the way exactly that you taught me to do, and I killed the wolf with one shot. It is the first time in my life that ever I have shot a gun and killed something. It is a grand thing, Señor Flint! I feel like I am king!'

Flint's face was impassive as he too knelt, raising his rifle to his shoulder. 'Crow later,' he barked at the jubilant Amado. 'There's others still killin' sheep.'

The death of the one wolf had not deterred the other three in any way. In fact, they seemed totally oblivious to anything except the surfeit of blood that had them crazed beyond reason or restraint.

Flint's rifle barked and a second wolf yelped and dropped. The rifle barked again, almost before the echoes of the first shot had bounced from the surrounding hills. A third wolf disappeared from sight amid the wooly sea of animals.

Amado contained his excitement and swung his rifle toward the remaining wolf. He found it in the sights and had started to tighten his finger on the trigger when Flint's rifle roared a third time. The wolf disappeared from Amado's sights.

Amado lifted his head from his rifle in confusion. 'Where did it go?' he breathed.

'Down.'

'Oh.'

'I don't see any more.'

'No. The sheep are still afraid, but not so much now that the wolves are not moving and killing.'

Flint shook his head. 'I always thought wolves only

killed to eat. I never heard of such a thing. They were just killin' as fast as they could kill.'

'*Sí, señor*. It is the way of wolves. They are not a nice animal. They will kill, even a very large animal, because they go in packs. When there is nothing left there to kill, they will eat until they cannot stand up. Then they sleep. Then they get up and go look for something else to kill. They will not even eat the same animal they have killed already, if they can find something new to kill instead. It is like it is their job, just to kill.'

Flint surprised himself by having to stifle the words: *just like me.*

The words so nearly spoken startled him. *Now why would I think like that?* he scolded himself silently.

But deep down, he knew why. Because it was the truth.

Renaldo trotted up to stand beside them, still breathing heavily from his earlier run, then running again to catch up to them. He looked out across the valley. Four wolves lay unmoving, surrounded by white piles of wool stained red with blood. He removed his hat. He struck his leg several times with the hat, while he ran his other hand across his head. 'My sheeps. My sheeps. They have kill so many of my sheeps. And my dog. My poor dog. He was so good with the sheeps. How will I take care of my sheeps without my dog?'

'What'll ya do now?' Flint asked.

Amado shrugged. 'I will stay here and help Renaldo. We will skin out all of the sheep that are dead. Their hide . . . no, it is . . . a moment, Señor

86

Flint. I will think of it. Fleece! Their fleeces will be worth moneys to Señora Burton. We will take as much of the meat as we can to the ranch for to eat. That is all we can do.'

Flint eyed what must have been more than twenty dead sheep. Terrified by the smell of blood, the other sheep had crowded back and moved off. The whole flock was moving, grazing the grass almost to bare ground as they did so.

The thought of helping the herders with their grisly task crossed his mind. Other things sounded much more appealing. 'I 'spect I'll ride on inta town,' he said.

Neither herder said anything, nor turned to watch him ride away. They were already busy with the unwelcome job before them.

CHAPTER 11

The town was unusually quiet. Nobody walked the sidewalks from business to business. No buggies or buckboards were tied up along the main street. Even the feed and grain store, usually the scene of bustling activity, was silent. A buckboard was backed up to the loading platform that ran along one side. Its team stamped restlessly in the quiet heat. They were the only things that moved.

Flint frowned. He had noticed the ripple that his appearance in town had caused. He hadn't thought it more than the usual effect of his presence.

It hadn't taken him that long to put his horse in a stall in the livery barn, measure out a half a gallon of oats, fill the manger with hay, pump a bucket of water for his water-trough, and re-enter the street.

Just that quickly, the street had changed. Fifteen minutes, he decided. Maybe twenty. A town switched from a busy cow-town to a ghost town in fifteen minutes.

He looked left and right. To his right and across the street, he guessed at least fifteen horses were in the vicinity of Bub's saLoon. The cowboy hangout.

The ranchers' turf. The enemy.

He almost smiled at that. How many times had he been on the other side of the fence? He'd never hired out to sheep-ranchers before. He had a natural affinity for cowmen, and the hard life they led. He understood their struggles against Indians, rustlers, land-grabbers, even the railroads. He had been involved in a number of those conflicts.

In the course of those conflicts he'd made some bitter enemies. He'd also made some close friends. For a while. Until the conflict was over. But they, like him, were drawn to the next conflict, the next job. They always went their separate ways when the job was done.

He thought of them from time to time. Each time they crossed his mind he wondered if this one or that one were still alive. They were probably dead, for the most part. There was always a faster gun, a quicker hand, a luckier lawman. Those who lived by their gun died by somebody else's. It was just the way of things.

He had long since resigned himself to the same fate. He had no way to know when, or where, or at whose hand, but he knew that one day he'd feel the slam of the bullet that would take his life.

He didn't mind the thought. It beat getting old and stove up, standing up with effort, living with pain, sleeping in fits between being wakened by aching joints. It sure beat getting old and lonely. Better to go out in a hail of gunfire than dwindle away in a fog of whiskey that never really dulled the loneliness or chased away the memories.

He had a lot of those memories. They started in the war. That was when he realized what a knack he had with a gun. After the war, he had honed, enhanced, nurtured that knack to a level of skill no one had been able to match. Yet. He practiced constantly to keep his skill at its deadly best.

That skill was quickly legendary among the hands of every ranch he had worked for. Cowboys and would-be gunmen had alike marveled at his speed and skill, and asked for pointers, instruction, help with their own skills.

Adamantly he had refused the endless requests. He wasn't a teacher. He did his job. He allowed no friendship, no loyalty, no emotion ever to get in the way. He didn't dare. He could not, dare not, allow himself to care. If the hard shell he had erected around his emotions ever cracked, he would be a dead man. He knew it as certainly as he knew what he was.

But still, there was that affinity for the hard-working, hard-fighting, hard-drinking, fun-loving, wild cowboys. They risked their lives for thirty a month and keep, dreamed endlessly of the little ranch they'd never own, and would stand and die for the brand for which they rode. He had to admit he liked most of them. Now, suddenly, the cowmen were 'the enemy.'

He shrugged inwardly. Well, that was just the way it was. Business was business. It wasn't his place to try to figure out who was right and who was wrong. He wasn't a judge. He was just a man who was very good at his job, doing the job he'd been hired to do.

So far, the score was impressive. He had sent nine of their erstwhile champions to an early grave. Ten, counting the one Amado's knife had dispatched. Eleven, if he included the hapless cowboy who fell victim to the small gunman's dying spasm. By his standards, he hadn't done all that much yet, but rumors indicated that already the ranchers were running scared. They were hiring as many gunfighters as they could find and import. Now, according to rumors that seemed to drift like tumbleweeds across the range, some of those hired gunmen were fighting amongst themselves. The ranchers had to move quickly, or they would self-destruct at the hands of the 'help' they had brought in to bolster their strength.

He had ridden into town today on a whim. A whim and a revulsion against skinning dead sheep. He wondered suddenly how Betty would react to what had happened. Without knowing why, he was certain her first concern would be for the faithful dog her herder had lost. He knew how vital a good dog was to a herder trying to control and contain that large a flock of sheep. He knew, as well, how close herder and dog became, isolated for months at a time with only each other. The campjack, who came about every third day to move the herder's wagon to a new bed-ground, usually came and went while he was with the sheep, so he didn't even get to talk with him. Now, without a dog, he was completely alone. Betty would know that. It would be her greatest concern. He didn't know why he knew that. It was just there, with absolute certainty, as soon as he thought about it.

He glanced along the street toward Shorty's – the saloon frequented by the sheepmen and their allies. Two horses idly swished their tails at the ever-present flies. There would probably be three or four herders inside as well, who had hitched a ride to town with someone. Unarmed, most likely, except for their knives.

He frowned. The idea of catching one or two of the ranchers' hired guns in town had been his only motivation for coming here. Had he misjudged? Had he already used that tactic one too many times? Had they figured out that they needed to come to town in groups, instead of one or two? Or three, he thought, with a tight smile.

He didn't like to go against three. He wasn't too fond of facing two, although it had never been a problem. It was close once. Really close. That was in Dodge City. That was a long time ago.

A knot in his gut told him he had walked into something he couldn't see. Whatever it was had to be a threat to his life. He considered backing into the livery barn. In his mind he resaddled his horse, eased out the back door of the livery barn, skirted as much of the town as possible, and headed out of town.

Angry at himself for the moment of indecision, he shook his head. He leaned against the side of the door, staring up the street. He fished out the makings and rolled himself a cigarette. He struck a match against the side of the door-frame and lit it, staring through the smoke, trying to think of a way to lure one or two of the gunmen away from Bub's.

He knew it would be suicide to beard the lion in its

den twice. He had escaped once, leaving Henshaw dead on the floor in his wake. He wasn't about to push his luck that far again.

He wondered suddenly where the cat was. He had used the animal to flush out whoever happened to be in Bub's. It had worked beautifully. It yielded the trio he had faced and killed. He wondered abruptly whether the cowboy – the one the gunman had gut-shot as he died – had survived. Right behind the memory, another thought foreign to his persona welled up in his mind. An instant of guilt and sympathy for the animal was immediately brushed aside. 'Gettin' like some old woman, worryin' about a danged cat,' he scolded himself.

Some cowboy started out the door of Bub's, spotted Flint, and jerked back. In less than half a minute, three others walked out through the door, single file.

All hired guns, Flint assessed silently.

He threw his cigarette onto the ground and ground it out with a boot-heel. He walked out to the center of the street. No words were spoken. There was no pretense. They all knew why they were all there. That they had been waiting for Flint was immediately obvious.

What was less obvious was just how prepared they were. As if on some silent signal, three others stepped out of the space between two buildings, across from Flint, and slightly to his left.

The knot in Flint's gut lurched and tightened. It was a trap. They had been waiting, maybe for days, knowing he was due to make another foray into town. He had used the same strategy one too many times.

As the realization settled into him, two more gunmen stepped from an opening between stores on the same side of the street he was on. That made eight. Eight to one.

The knot in his gut relaxed abruptly. In its place an icy calm spread, coursing through him, leaving him devoid of any feeling. His mind began to race. Knowing his own death was imminent and unavoidable, he shifted to trying to figure the best way to take as many as possible with him. He made a swift mental assessment of each man facing him. Guessing at their relative speed, he formed a plan that would make his first four shots as rapid as ever he was capable.

Four. Maybe. If he was lucky. If he had chosen accurately. That left four, whose guns would certainly be barking his death-knell by the time his own fourth shot was loosed. Maybe sooner than that.

Maybe, just maybe, he could stand and chalk up one more before the bullets ripping into him forced him to the ground. He had seen men do it before. He watched a man, once, keep firing when he had seven bullets in him. He was dead when he hit the ground, but he had stood long enough to kill his attackers. With no emotion whatever he wondered if he would be able to do as well. He hoped he lived long enough to know, before the darkness swept him away.

One of the gunmen spoke, his voice affable. 'We finally meet, Flint.'

'Do I know you?'

'Nope. I heard of you, though.'

'That so?'

'Down at Laredo. Year an' a half ago. I heard ya took out Vance Spaulding an' Kid Hofer at the same time. I knew 'em both. Fast. Ya really outdrew 'em both together, like I heard?'

'I'm here. They ain't.'

'I heard ya got three of Overhostler's boys at once here, t'other day. Stark an' the twins. I seen Stark in action, too. Used too little a gun, but fast. Real fast.'

'Not fast enough.'

The gunman grinned. His face lit up with the grin. It seemed as open and honest as a schoolboy's, as if he'd never had a serious moment in his life. 'Then I don't suppose I am either. But it don't matter, today. You just went an' walked into one you ain't gonna walk out of. I don't care how fast you are, you ain't good enough to take out eight of us.'

'You boys all work for Overhostler?'

The gunman grinned again. 'Sure. You got him awful riled up. The rest o' the ranchers, too. Now it's just you, all by yourself, against eight of us. I guess we could be real sportin', an' let you go for your gun first.'

'The odds ain't too good,' Flint agreed.

'They're just perfect.' The gunman grinned. 'Eight of us, and only one of you.'

A voice from behind the trio froze everyone. 'You forgot to count me. I make two.'

The happy gunman's smile faded. He turned his head. The one who stood in the middle of the street, hand just touching the worn walnut handles of a Colt .45, was cut from the same cloth as the other gunmen. Yet, there was something different. It wasn't arrogance, but close. He exuded an air of calm confidence, as if he thought he could take the other eight by himself.

The smile was gone from the spokesman's face. 'Who are you?'

'Does it matter?'

'This ain't your party.'

'Don't be too sure. That fella you're fixin' to use for target practice is a friend o' mine. I ain't seen 'im since one time down along the Cimarron, but we shot up a whole bunch o' guys down there that was better gunmen than I 'spect you'll ever be.'

'Who are you?' the gunman demanded again.

'Name's Bill Jeffers, if that matters.'

It mattered. That it mattered was reflected in every face on the street. The gunmen in a half-circle around Flint began to glance at one another, then at the newcomer. That the odds were still four to one didn't seem that reassuring.

Yet another gunman stepped out from between the buildings three of the gunmen had appeared from. He was directly behind that trio. That fact, also, was not lost on any of them when he spoke.

'Howdy, Flint.'

Flint carefully concealed his surprise and resisted the urge to smile. 'Howdy Red,' he responded.

He turned to the cheerful gunman who seemed to be the self-appointed spokesman of the ranchers' gun hands. 'What did you say your name was?'

The gunman's head acted momentarily as if his neck were a swivel, trying to look at all three of his adversaries at the same time. 'Art,' he said, almost biting off the words. 'Art Halfheid.'

'Well, Art, what were you sayin' about me bein' in a spot? It sorta seems ta me that we got you boys pretty well surrounded.'

Art turned to the gunman beside him. 'I thought you told me Flint was the only one the sheepmen had the money ta hire!'

The man he addressed swallowed with difficulty. 'That's what Overhostler told me.'

Red spoke to Flint. 'Oscar an' Herman are up on roofs. You say the word, an' we'll open the festivities here.'

Every one of the ranchers' gunmen reacted instantly. Eyes jerked to the roofs along the main street, straining for some indication of the hidden allies of their intended victim. That things had swung dramatically out of their control was an understatement of gigantic proportions. With their darting eyes and fidgeting, they began to look like a group of cornered rats, looking desperately for any possible avenue of escape.

Flint addressed the gunman whose smile had long since disappeared. 'Looks ta me like you boys is the ones that stumbled into a tight spot.'

Unexpectedly, the gunman's grin lit up his face again. 'Well now, I guess I can't argue with that,' he agreed. 'Dangdest thing I ever heard of. The question is, what now? Are we gonna have us one shoot-'em-up Jim-dandy of a circus here, or can we cut a deal?'

Hope flared in Flint, even though his face remained totally impassive. 'What kind o' deal ya got in mind?'

'Well, what if we all offer ta cut an' run? We ride outa the country, an' leave you boys ta deal with the ranchers however you're a mind to?'

'I'd sooner do that than die in the street here, provin' how brave I am,' a second gunman offered, speaking for the first time.

'Same goes for me,' a third chimed in.

It took Flint less time to make a decision than it did for him to voice it. 'Your horses are right over there.'

It was all the eight needed. In less time than it would have taken to reload a pistol, all eight were in the saddle, heading out of town at a fast trot.

CHAPTER 12

The three stood like statues until the eight gunmen faded into a blur behind the cloud of dust their horses stirred. Then Flint strode forward. An unaccustomed smile erased the hardness from his face. 'Bill! Red! What are you boys doin' here?'

'Heard you was raisin' Cain up here. Thought you might need some help,' Bill replied, striding forward to grasp Flint's hand in a long, firm grip. The same ritual was exchanged wordlessly between Flint and Red.

'How'd ya hear that?' Flint queried.

Red spoke for the first time. 'We was in Amarillo. Just finished up a little business over in the Indian Nation. Fella came along offerin' work fer fellas good with a gun. We jawed with 'im a while. Turns out he was sent by one o' the ranchers here – U-Cross ranch, I think – Ulysses J. Hodges' outfit. Offered a hundred-dollar up-front bonus, a hundred a month an' keep, an' only one gunman on t' other side ta even need ta worry about.'

'Hirin' everybody they can, huh?'

'Seems that way,' Bill agreed. 'Didn't seem just

right, somehow. Why would somebody be hirin' all the gun hands he can find, just to go against a bunch o' Mexican sheepherders an' one lone gunman. So we sorta asked who that one fella was that they was so scared of.'

'You got quite a reputation goin',' Red inserted. 'He said you'd already took out about half a dozen of his best gunmen.'

'The odds didn't sound too good,' Bill explained. 'We decided maybe we'd oughta even 'em up just a tad. We told the fella "No, thanks," then we rode fast enough ta blow off most of our stink gettin' here.'

'Your timin' couldn'ta been better,' Flint observed. 'I'd just decided it was checkin' out time, an' figurin' out how ta take as many with me as I could.'

'I 'spect you could've gotten off about three shots while you rolled back into the livery barn,' Bill suggested. 'That would've given you some cover, you in there where it's sorta dark an' them out in the sun.'

'I'd thought of that,' Flint admitted. 'I was arguin' with myself whether to do that or just stand an' blaze away. See if I could keep standin' long enough to take most of 'em with me at least.'

'Which side o' that argument was winnin'?'

'Headin' for cover,' Flint admitted. 'I liked the idea o' goin' out in a blaze o' glory, but since I'm the only thing standin' 'twixt the sheep outfits an' all the ranchers' hired guns, I decided I'd oughta see if maybe I could keep breathin' a while.'

'You really are the only gun hand the sheepmen got?'

'I'm it.'

'Why? I mean, why would you agree to somethin' like that? That ain't like the Flint I know.'

Flint thought about it for several minutes. 'I ain't real sure. I took their up-front money without knowin' the whole story. But I did give my word.'

'Givin' your word when ya been flamboozled ain't a bindin' promise,' Red asserted.

Flint's nod indicated agreement his words belied. 'I know, but I did. Then, there's a situation er two I just couldn't make myself ride away from.'

'What kinda situation?'

'Well, the outfit where I'm stayin' is ramrodded by a woman whose man was killed by the ranchers. They figured she'd cut 'n run, soon as he was gone. She didn't. She's the one that scraped up the money to hire me.'

'Good-lookin' widow?'

Flint fought against the flushing he felt invade his face. 'That ain't it at all! It's just . . . I just didn't like the way the whole situation . . . well, yeah, she is. It ain't that, though. She wouldn't have nothin' ta do with a gunman like me.'

Silence hung in the street for several seconds. 'So you really are the only one, huh?'

'I'm it.'

'Sounds like you could use a little help.'

Flint took a deep breath. 'Yeah, I could that. Trouble is, they ain't got no money ta pay you boys.'

Red and Bill exchanged a look. It was Red who explained. 'We figured that out before we left Amarillo. We'd both've been dead a couple times at

101

least, if it wasn't for you. We figured we owe you one. We thought we'd just throw in with you, instead o' sittin' around drinkin' up all the wages we made from the last outfit.'

'You'd work for nothin'?'

'We owe ya.'

'Folks die tryin' ta pay back that kinda debt,' Flint asserted. ' 'Specially gun hands.'

'Gotta die sometime.' Bill shrugged.

'What about Oscar an' Herman?' Flint asked suddenly.

Red laughed aloud. Bill just grinned. It was Bill who answered. 'Fact is, Oscar went an' got himself killed in the Indian Nation. Herman ended up on the wrong end of an affair in Kansas. He went an' got himself hung.'

Red continued the explanation. 'I just thought tellin' you they was up on the roof'd cause a couple o' them boys ta wet their pants.'

'It worked.' Flint grinned. 'They was plumb anxious ta ride outa town.'

'You think they left the country?'

Flint shook his head. 'Oh, there might be one or two who will. The rest'll change their minds as soon as they think about it. We'll still have 'em ta deal with.'

'So what kinda plan ya got?'

'Well, I been teachin' the herders ta use a rifle.'

Red and Bill exchanged a look. Bill said: 'You're teachin' Greasers to shoot?'

Flint shrugged. 'They pick it up in a hurry. We ain't got rifles for 'em all, but they're all learnin'.'

'You're teachin' Greasers to shoot!' Bill said again.

'You're goin' soft,' Red accused. 'Never thought I'd see the day.'

'Somebody comin',' Bill said.

Red and Flint jerked their eyes to the direction Bill was watching. A cloud of dust approached the town, still the better part of a mile away. 'Gotta be three or four,' Red surmised. 'Runnin' their horses plumb hard.'

'In a hurry, that's for sure,' Flint agreed.

Wordlessly the trio walked to the livery barn and stepped back into the shadows of its interior to watch and wait.

They didn't have long to wait. In minutes Ian Flanders, Cowp Smith, his foreman, and Juan Rigalado, one of his herders, thundered into town. They skidded their horses to a stop in front of Shorty's. They looked around in obvious confusion.

Flint stepped from the livery barn. 'Howdy, Mr Flanders.'

Flanders stared at Flint, then looked around at the rest of the town. 'What happened?' he demanded.

Flint feigned total ignorance. 'Was somethin' supposed to happen?'

Flander's confusion almost left him unable to speak. 'I thought . . . I heard . . . Juan come out home ridin' hell for leather, sayin' the ranchers' gun fighters had set up a trap for you here in town. He said there was eight or ten of 'em.'

Flint shrugged. 'Just eight.'

'Just eight? Just eight? What happened?'

'I just offered ta let 'em all ride out instead o'

tryin' ta take me on, if they wanted to. They just all rode out.'

It was all Flint could do to keep from laughing. The big sheep-rancher's face was a comedy of passing emotions and confusion as he tried to digest what Flint had said. That it was ridiculous went without saying. But where were the ranchers' gunmen? Where were signs of any battle? There were no bodies, no blood in the street, no lingering smell of gunpowder.

'That don't make no sense,' he said.

It was the first time the sheepman had ever seen Flint smile. 'The fact is, I sorta had some help. Come on out, boys.'

Red and Bill stepped out to stand beside Flint. 'Mr Flanders, this here's Bill Jeffers an' Red Saxon. Red's the one that ain't got brown hair. They're friends o' mine. They rode up from Texas ta see if they could help out a bit. What I said about the ranchers' gun hands was true, but it was Red an' Bill bein' here that made 'em see the wisdom o' that.'

Flanders studied the trio for half a minute, then said: 'This is a story I gotta hear. Let's see if Shorty's got somethin' to wash the dust outa our throats with. You can see if you can clear up this cloud o' confusion I seem ta be in the middle of here.'

That sounded like a really good idea to all of them.

CHAPTER 13

'So how'd you get the name "Cowp"?' Bill asked abruptly.

They had been in the quiet cool interior of Shorty's for nearly half an hour. The story of how Bill and Red had arrived to even out the odds and thwart the intentions of the ranchers had been told, marveled at, and laughed over.

Cowp shrugged his shoulders. 'It's just easier'n my whole name.'

'So what's your whole name?'

'Cowperthwaite Harrington Smith.'

The others stared at him in dumbfounded disbelief. It was Red who said: 'You're puttin' us on!'

Cowp sipped his beer. 'Nope. God's truth.'

'Why would anyone hang a moniker like that on a poor defenseless kid?' Bill probed.

Cowp chuckled. 'My ma didn't much like the name Smith. Said it was too plain, lacking any distinction. If a man is to achieve in life, he needs a name of distinction. So she thought up something truly distinguished. She wouldn't let anybody call me "Cowp" either. It was the full name, or face her wrath.'

'Left home when ya was six, I bet,' Bill observed.

'Fifteen,' Cowp corrected.

Their conversation was interrupted by an unexpected visitor. He slid in the back door of Shorty's almost like a shadow. His too-big trousers hung on twin pieces of twine that looped up over his bony shoulders. He held a tattered old rag of a hat in both hands as he glanced around nervously.

Spotting the table at which Flint, Flanders and the others were talking, he sidled toward them. He cast furtive glances around the room as he approached, as though fearful some dreadful thing might attack him at any moment.

'Mr Flanders?' he apologized as he approached the table.

Flanders responded immediately, breaking off what he was saying to Flint in mid-sentence. 'Why, Skinny! How are you? I haven't seen you around lately. You working someplace, are you?'

Skinny bobbed his head. 'Sure am, Mr Flanders. I ain't gonna be available for lambin' next year, I'm afraid.'

'Aw, that's too bad,' Flanders offered. 'I always look forward to your help. You're a good hand with sheep.'

'Thank you, Mr Flanders. I've always liked sheep. I just can't handle the work no more. My rheumatism's just too bad these days. I been workin' for Mr Steinberg at the mercantile store, when the weather ain't too damp. He lets me stay in the shed out back in the summer, and lets me sleep in the cellar in winter. The cellar's damp on my rheumatism, but it's warm enough.'

'I'm glad to hear you're cared for, Skinny. What brings you here?'

Skinny cast another furtive glance around the room, to be sure no extra ears were listening. He lowered his nasal voice, making it difficult to hear. Flint leaned forward to catch his words. 'You always treated me good, Mr Flanders. You always paid me good for what help I could be lambin'. I got no use for most o' the cattlemen. High an' mighty, they are. Just as soon spit on me as speak to me.'

'Like I said, you were always as good help as your health would let you be.'

'I just heard Mr Steinberg talkin' to Gabe Kilmer, him as runs the Circle J. Kilmer ordered three cases o' Winchester 73s, an' a case o' .50 caliber Sharps rifles, along with four cases o' ammunition for the Winchesters an' two cases for the Sharps.'

The men at the table looked at each other in unabashed astonishment as silence hung in the air, dangling from the old-timer's words. It was Flint who brushed aside the astonishment and began to ask questions.

'Where they getting 'em, old-timer?'

Skinny licked his lips. 'They telegraphed the order back East. Havin' 'em shipped to the end o' the railroad at Laramie. They're sendin' two o' Kilmer's gun hands down with a buckboard on the tenth to pick 'em up an' haul 'em back here.'

Flint leaned back, his mind racing. 'Well, whatd'ya know,' he crooned. 'Whatd'ya know! Now that's a piece of news.'

He turned to Skinny. 'Listen, old-timer, you better be sure the ranchers don't know you told anyone.'

The old man shook his head vigorously. 'Oh, there ain't no danger o' that. I'm old an' crippled up, but I ain't lost my mind. No siree. I only come over on account o' Mr Flanders always treated me right. 'Sides, I got no use for Kilmer. No siree, I sure ain't gonna never let on I even knowed nothin' about it. I gotta go now, afore someone spots me in here.'

Flint reached into his pocket and fished out a twenty-dollar gold piece. Palming it, he held out his hand to the old man. 'Thank you, Skinny. I think you've just repaid Mr Flanders for everything he's done for you.'

As he shook the old man's hand he pressed the gold piece into his palm. The old man's eyes flew wide for just an instant, then moistened perceptibly. He bobbed his head once and whirled, sidling out the back door as furtively as he had entered.

'Gotta be hard, gettin' old an' crippled up with no family or nothin',' Bill observed.

'He was a good man once,' Flanders agreed.

'He still is,' Flint disagreed. 'He just ain't got much body left to keep that good man goin'.'

'So the ranchers are armin' for an all-out war,' Flanders mused.

'They got enough guns an' ammunition already for that,' Flint disagreed.

The others frowned at him. Flanders put their

confusion into words. 'You think they're up to some-thin' else?'

'Gotta be,' Flint affirmed. 'They got guns an' ammunition enough to kill us all, if they get the chance.'

'Well, it sounds like they're about to get a whole lot more.'

'Couldn't be more perfect,' Flint observed.

The others stared at him, eyebrows arched. 'What are you thinkin'?' Bill asked, when no explanation was forthcoming.

'Well, the herders have been learnin' to shoot pretty well. All they need is rifles. We got about forty more herders than we have rifles. Now we find out that a whole shipment of rifles, including some Sharps for long-range work, are just about to be provided for us.'

The others at the table exchanged quick glances. Red started to grin. 'You ain't just by chance plannin' on divertin' one particular buckboard to a different destination, are you?'

Flint grinned back. 'Seems like a good idea at the time. Listen. The tenth is only three days away. That gives us four days after that to get the rifles passed out to all the herders who can shoot. That's almost all of 'em, now. Then we gotta take everyone we can to bring that other six thousand head o' sheep here.'

Red and Bill looked at each other. Red asked: 'What six thousand sheep?'

'Oh, I guess I hadn't told you boys about that. It seems there's six thousand head o' sheep bein' shipped to the railhead. They'll arrive there the sixteenth.'

'You're gonna bring six thousand head o' sheep into the middle of a range war?'

'The sheep-ranchers figured that would be the straw that would break the cattlemen's back. They'd know the sheep-ranchers are serious about stayin'.'

Bill leaned back in his chair. 'And the ranchers just happened to order forty Winchesters and twenty Sharps rifles, and about twenty thousand rounds of ammunition. You don't suppose, just by chance, that they plan the same sort of thing with them sheep that we plan with the rifles, do you?'

Flanders' face paled noticeably. 'You think they know?'

Flint snorted. 'Dumber'n I think they are if they don't. Why do you think I was so mad when Betty told me about it. That many sheep will move slower'n molasses in January. They'll be sittin' ducks for cowboys or gun hands, either one, to sit along the hills an' pick 'em off. You think wolves kill a lot o' sheep. Even they get tired enough so they can't kill any more, eventually. Rifles don't get tired. Rifles do wear out. Especially when you're shootin' as fast as you can, slaughterin' a bunch o' sheep. That's why they gotta have a lot more rifles, so when the barrel wears out on one, that guy can just grab a new one. They can keep shootin' till six thousand sheep are as dead as the ones herdin' 'em. Then they can go from ranch to ranch an' do the same with every flock o' sheep on the range.'

Flanders blanched as Flint talked. 'So what are your plans?' he demanded.

Flint's eyes actually twinkled for an instant as he began to lay out his plan.

CHAPTER 14

'You can never always sometimes tell.'

'What?'

'I said, "You can never—" '

'I heard what you said. It just doesn't make any sense.'

'Neither does the rest of life, most of the time.'

Betty stared at him, undecided whether to be angry or laugh. 'I just asked what you thought the ranchers would try to do next. But if you really want to know, it isn't only your life that doesn't make sense,' she said at last.

He was far more aware of her closeness than he would have wanted to admit. He wanted to move away, to stop the feelings that kept surging through him. At the same time he didn't want the feelings to stop. Trying hard to ignore those feelings, he said: 'What else don't make sense?'

She looked up into his eyes. 'Why would two professional gunfighters offer to come here and help us, just out of the kindness of their hearts?'

'They owe me.' He shrugged.

'And did you ask them to come?'

He shook his head. 'I wasn't even sure they were still alive. Anyhow, I wouldn't ask.'

'So they just came because they heard you were in trouble?'

'Sorta like that, I guess.'

'And you would do the same for them?'

It was a new idea to him. He had never even come close to thinking about such a thing before. He knew the answer, though, quite a while before he dared to put it into words. That he did put it into words – that he admitted it – came as a surprise even to him. 'Yeah.'

She stared at him for a long moment, then asked: 'And do I need to be on my guard because these two professional gunfighters are also staying in my bunkhouse? I have never considered gunfighters to be men of high moral character. Will they bother me?'

Surprise, then anger flared briefly in his eyes. 'Of course not! You don't think I'd let 'em on the place if I figured they were any threat to you, do you?'

'Are you telling me that you're protecting me?'

'Well, sure. I told 'em you was way off limits. They know if they even say anything outa line ta you, they'll answer ta me. They wouldn't neither one do nothin' like that anyway. Red an' Bill are both good men.'

Ignoring the last of what he said, she narrowed the focus of her questioning. 'And just what gives you the idea that you have any right to be the defender of my honor? Did you tell them that there was anything between us other than a strictly business arrangement?'

113

Taken aback, he stammered: 'No! 'Course not! No. I just . . . well, they asked, that's all. I told them there wasn't nothin' between us.'

He took a deep breath. In a less flustered, but suddenly flat voice, he continued! 'I told 'em you were one fine woman. I told 'em that you were the only woman I'd ever met that made me think about ever doin' somethin' besides what I do. Too fine a woman to ever have any interest in the likes o' me. But that didn't give them no free rein ta bother you. You don't have to worry.'

Her anger melted away, leaving an expression in her eyes he couldn't begin to fathom. The moment was shattered and whisked away by the soft voice of Bill Jeffers. 'There's another thing or two he ain't tellin' you, ma'am.'

She whirled to look at the gunman, annoyance at the interruption giving a sharp edge to her voice. 'And what is that?' she demanded.

Bill smiled. 'This here fella you hired is a whole lot more man than he'll be willin' to tell you. Me'n Red are both here because we know what it's like to be in a situation that's certain death. Flint put his own life on the line twice for the two of us. Saved our skins, when he didn't have no reason in the world to do it. I 'spect he's still carryin' three or four bullets because of it.'

Her eyes whipped back to Flint, wide with both concern and surprise. 'You did that?'

'Bill, you talk too much,' Flint protested.

'Somebody needs ta tell it. You won't,' Bill responded.

He turned again to Betty. 'One time was down along the Cimarron. A couple o' outfits down there that was more outlaw and rustler gangs than legitimate ranchers was gangin' up on a bunch o' little guys. Some of 'em small ranchers. Some of 'em homesteaders. They pooled their money an' hired the three of us ta sorta even out the odds a mite. Me'n Red stumbled into a trap they'd laid for us. We was goners fer sure, just tryin' ta hold out as long as we could. Then here comes Flint, ridin' hell fer leather, holdin' the reins of 'is horse in 'is teeth, blazin' away from a dead run with both o' them guns o' his, racin' back an' forth along behind the ones that had us pinned down. He sent a dozen of them ba ... uh, them ... fellas to the promised land all by hisself. Got shot up some doin' it, but the ones that still could split an' run, an' me'n Red lived to fight another day.'

'You talk too much,' Flint protested again.

'Then there was one other time,' Bill continued, but was interrupted before he could continue with that story.

'Someone comin'',' Flint barked. His gun was in his hand as he stepped between Betty and the rider coming on a dead run.

Andy Sparks, Betty's only white herder, skidded his horse to a stop in a cloud of dust. 'Flint!' he yelled. 'Amado an' Gregorio spotted a bunch o' cowboys headin' toward the big valley. There's seven of 'em, an' they all got a bag o' somethin' tied onto their saddles. Two of 'em look to be gunfighters.'

'What on earth could they be doing?' Betty frowned.

There was no answer for a long moment, as each probed their thoughts for possibilities. Flint and Bill hit the same thought at the same time. Their heads jerked up, their eyes telegraphing to each other the realization that had just dawned in their minds.

'Where were they?'

'Just about three miles below the valley. They're ridin' slow. Them bags bounce around if they try to speed up, so they're ridin' at a walk.'

Flint turned to Andy. 'That valley's got the big spring-fed pond at the upper end, don't it?'

Andy nodded, frowning. 'Yeah. That's what makes it such good grazin' for the sheep. The pond's fed by half a dozen springs, and a flock o' sheep can water there indefinitely.'

'What'd happen if someone poured, say, about two or three hundred pounds of strychnine into it, where the water comes in from the springs.'

Andy's eyes went wide. He swore. 'It'd kill pertn-eart the whole flock o' sheep. When sheep are waterin' there, they just about keep up with the springs, so no water'd run out. The poison'd stay right there till the sheep drank it. Sheep ain't like them danged coyotes. It don't take a big dose o' strychnine to kill a sheep, like it does coyotes.'

Flint turned to Bill. 'We gotta head 'em off. If we cut straight across, we oughta get to the pond well ahead of 'em.'

He turned to Andy. 'Get yourself a fresh horse an' get back to Amado an' Gregorio. Have 'em meet us in the rocks just west o' the pond. If the cowboys get there before we do, have 'em open up on 'em. Do

116

they both have rifles?'

Andy nodded. 'So do I.'

'Then have 'em open up on 'em before they can dump any o' them bags. Have 'em shoot for the bags. If they hit a bag, it'll make a hole an' get rid o' the strychnine, even if they don't stop 'em. It'll give 'em a thing or two to think about till we get there.'

Without waiting to reply, Andy turned his horse toward the barn to change mounts. He had barely left the barn on the fresh horse before Flint and Bill followed in his wake, riding hard.

Betty stood in the yard, trying to sort out a hundred emotions flooding her mind.

CHAPTER 15

Their horses were lathered, breathing heavily. Foam dangled from the ends of their bits, to be blown away by the wind of their speed. Flint was nearly a quarter-mile ahead of the rest by the time they neared the head of the big valley. He reined his horse to a swift trot, listening intently. No sound broke the silence of the deepening twilight.

He rode to a large clump of brush and small trees he thought was within a hundred yards of the slope, covered with talus and boulders, leading down to the spring-fed pond. He dismounted and tied the reins to a small tree. He looked his horse over, struggling with the need to rub the animal down after such a hard run. He glanced toward where Amado, Gregorio and possibly the herder should be waiting. If they were still alive. If he weren't already too late.

Swiftly he ripped open his bedroll, whipped out two blankets and draped them over the lathered gelding, then started for the edge of the brush.

Bill Jeffers and Andy Sparks braked their horses from a run as they entered the copse. Not bothering to pamper their mounts, they jerked rifles from saddle scabbards and followed Flint.

As he neared the rim of the rocky outcropping, Flint chanced an effort to find the others. 'Amado,' he said softly.

'Señor Flint?' the answer came immediately, in conversational tones.

'Yeah. Any sign of 'em?'

'No, *señor*. They were walking their horses slowly because of the bags they carry. I think they will not be here for maybe thirty minutes or perhaps an hour yet.'

'Good. That'll give us time to get set where we wanta be.'

'We are in a good position, Señor Flint. We are in very good range of the whole pond of water with our rifles, and we are all behind rocks that will make us very hard for them to shoot.'

'Where you at?'

'We are all three in the rocks right over here to the south of the water.'

'What's to stop them from scatterin' into the rocks over there as soon as they know you're here? Then they'll be in rocks just like you, so you lose the advantage.'

'*Por Dios*, Señor Flint! I did not even think of such a thing. I think I am not very good at this sort of affair.'

'You're not supposed to be. That's what we're here for.'

'Where is Señor Red, Señor Flint? I do not see him with you.'

'We left him to ride herd on the ranch, just in case

somebody decided it'd be a good time ta try some-thin' there. I didn't wanta leave Betty with nobody around.'

'I think you have come to think very much of our Señora, Señor Flint.'

Flint ignored the comment. 'Bill will stay here with you boys. Andy an' I'll go over along the other side, where we can keep the whole bunch o' them out in the open. It'll be dark by the time they get here, but there's a full moon already up, so we'll be able to see just fine.'

'Do you want that we shoot them all when they get here, Señor?'

Flint shook his head. 'Not if we can help it. I think there's only two gunfighters in the bunch. The rest are just cowboys, followin' orders. I have a hunch they ain't too keen on what they're doin', but they'll ride for the brand. When they see they're caught dead ta rights, they'll give it up in a hurry.'

'I think the gunfighters will not.'

'I 'spect you're right. We'll see. If shootin' starts, aim for the bags. I don't think even that much strych-nine'll do much harm lyin' on the ground. It'll soak in with the first rain an' be gone. If ya hit a bag, it'll leak out till it's empty. A bullet hittin' a bag will likely make the horse go plumb wild, an' the cowboys are goin' ta be doin' some real fancy ridin' just ta stay in the saddle.'

Amado' s grin lighted up his face. '*Sí, señor*!' he said with a look of gleeful anticipation.

It was just over half an hour later when they heard the first sounds of the cowboys' approach. There was no talk. A hoof clicked against a rock. A saddle squeaked. A horse blew noisily. Everyone in the rocks squirmed lower. Rifles were leveled across the top or along the edge of large boulders. Hats were laid aside to make them less visible.

The first rider to come into view was the gunman with the open grin, who had been the spokesman in the intended ambush of Flint in town. Flint swore silently as he recognized him

Behind him, riding single file, the others came into view. At the edge of the pond they stopped, spreading out as if by some perverse urge to arrange themselves perfectly for the hidden rifles among the rocks.

'Thought you promised ta ride outa the country, Art,' Flint called out in a conversational tone.

Every one in the group jumped as if some hidden charge of electricity had jolted through their bodies simultaneously. The other obvious gunfighter in the group swore. His gun was in his hand as if by magic, barking and sending rock chips flying around the source of Flint's voice.

Four rifles responded instantly. They were all well-aimed. Four slugs slammed into the gunman's chest at almost the same instant, driving him backward off his horse.

Several of the cowboys immediately raised their hands. Art sat stock still, his hands on the saddle horn.

One of the cowboys had maneuvered his horse at the first sound of Flint's voice, so he was sideways to those in the rocks. Furtively he worked his rifle up

121

out of the scabbard, on the side of his horse hidden from the herders. One of them noticed anyway.

Another rifle shot shattered the silence that followed the first gunman's death. The bag of silverish crystals dangling from the saddle just behind the cowboy began to pour out a steady stream of the substance. The horse squealed in pain and terror, both at the impact of the bullet against the bag, and the burning streak across its hide as the bullet passed through the bag and beyond. It began to whirl and buck furiously.

The cowboy dropped the rifle he had furtively withdrawn from the scabbard and grabbed the saddle horn, fighting desperately to keep his seat.

A second rifle shot perforated a bag on a second horse, and that animal, too, erupted in a terrified paroxysm of bucking, twisting, running, and fighting to get free of the restricting control of its rider.

Art turned to watch the impromptu bronc rides, grinning broadly, as if he were without a care in the world. The rest of the cowboys all had their hands high in the air now. One of them said: 'Don't go doin' that no more! You'll ruin my horse!'

The oddity of his greater concern for his mount than his own safety struck Flint. 'Hold your fire,' he called.

One of the two horses terrified by having the bags shot was slowly brought under control. The other succeeded in ridding himself of his rider and pounded away into the darkness at a dead run.

Flint turned his attention back to Art. He stepped out from the rocks and faced the gunman. 'I sorta thought even a gunfighter was bound by his word.'

Art stepped from his horse, still grinning. 'Well, now, I most generally am. Problem is, by the time we got back out to Overhostler's, I'd had a bit o' time to think. I was plumb mad about havin' a perfect set-up like that turned against me. Then Overhostler, he offered us double pay for a month if we'd stick around instead o' lightin' out. I just plumb had a change o' heart.'

'Then I don't guess there's much sense askin' for your word again.'

Art grinned again. 'Well now, I don't know about that. You see—'

In the middle of a word, hoping to catch Flint off guard, his hand streaked up from his holster holding the Colt .45 that had dispatched so many unwary adversaries.

Flint was not unwary. His own Russian .44 roared before Art's pistol had much more than cleared its holster. He took a step backward as the bullet slammed into him.

His gun, however, continued its rise until a second lead projectile pounded into him, driving the grin from his face and the life from his body. He collapsed to his knees, then toppled sideways. He lay with his head cradled in the arm that still gripped the gun he would never fire again.

Still holding the Russian .44, Flint addressed the now silent group of cowboys, all with their hands as high as they could reach. 'That's a lot o' somethin' you boys is carryin'. What is it?'

No answer was forthcoming. He pointed his

sidearm at the nearest cowboy. 'I asked a question. What is it?'

The cowboy started to answer, but only a croak emerged from his mouth. He cleared his throat and tried again. 'Strychnine. Overhostler put in a special order an' got four hundred pounds of it.'

'You boys ever watch an animal die o' strychnine poisonin'?'

Heads shook instantly, indicating that none of them had. 'It ain't a pretty way for anythin' ta die,' Flint said. 'I don't even like usin' it on coyotes an' wolves, even though it's gotta be done ta keep 'em from wipin' out ranchers. It sure ain't no way for sheep ta have ta die.'

The cowboy who had answered the question spoke again. 'I don't 'spect any of us is a bit proud o' bein' part o' this,' he said. 'We shoulda just quit the country instead. Trouble is, we'd likely get killed if we tried. Overhostler, he's gone plumb nuts with hate.'

'How about the other ranchers?'

That time the answer was slower coming. It was the same rider who eventually answered. 'I wouldn't be surprised if the others'd be halfway reasonable, if it wasn't for Overhostler. Him an' Kilmer. They purty well got the rest buffaloed.'

'You boys ready ta pass around a bag o' that stuff you was gonna feed the sheep? Seems fittin' you all oughta at least have a good taste of it.'

Even in the early moonlight, he could see every face blanch. A heretofore silent cowboy said: 'You wouldn't really do that, would ya? Make us eat that, I mean?'

'Why not? You thought it was good enough for a whole flock o' sheep.'

'Yeah, but . . . OK, I'll admit that's probably what we deserve, but there ain't no way I'm gonna die like that. If that's what you're determined ta do, I'll go fer my gun an' make ya kill me quick.'

'Then I guess you best all untie them bags an' let 'em drop. I ain't about ta let ya take it back for Overhostler ta send someone else out to poison the water-holes with it.'

As if a great rush of air abruptly exhaled from every rider, they hastened to untie the bags of crystalline powder and drop them to the ground.

'Now you best drop your guns alongside 'em,' Flint commanded.

They all complied at once.

'Now you got a choice. You can ride back and tell Overhostler what happened, or you can ride outa the country. If you stay on with Overhostler, and you end up facin' us again, I'll remember your faces. You won't ride away twice. Now get outa here.'

There was just an instant's hesitation. Then one of the cowboys said: 'Much obliged, Flint.'

They all wheeled their horses and cantered away.

CHAPTER 16

'You reckon that's them?'

'Gotta be.'

'I thought Skinny said there'd just be two guards with it. There's two on the buckboard an' two riders. That adds up to four in my book.'

'Prob'ly not all, either.'

Red's eyes jerked to Flint. 'What d'ya mean?'

Flint studied the distant wagon through the telescope for several minutes before answering. He lowered the telescope and looked at his friend. 'Well, they know we got wind o' the plan to poison the pond an' kill the whole band in the big valley. They gotta be wonderin' how we did that. They gotta be wonderin' if one o' their own is sellin' 'em out. If they are, they're gonna be wonderin' if we know about the rifles too.'

'So you think it might be some sort o' set-up?'

'Wouldn't you plan it that way, if you was them?'

It was Amado who answered. '*Sí*. It would be foolish to have so many guns and bullets to be guarded by only two men. Or even to have all its guards where we could see so easily.'

There were four of them as well. Flint was accompanied by Amado Martinez, Gregorio Jiminez and Red Saxon. Bill Jeffers and Andy Sparks had been left at the B-B sheep ranch to protect it and Betty.

'How do we find if it is true?' Gregorio asked softly.

'There!' Red said, raising a finger to point. 'In them trees. Hundred yards or so from the road.'

Flint raised the telescope and slowly scanned the patch of timber his friend indicated. 'What'd ya see?'

'Something moved. Sun caught somethin' for a second.'

'There he is! I see 'im. One o' Overhostler's gun hands. Sittin' in the trees, watchin' the buckboard.'

'There is another one on this side of the road, *amigo*,' Amado said, pointing.

Flint quickly confirmed the accuracy of the observation. Another of the gunfighters was trotting along, parallel to the road, about a hundred yards to the near side. As they watched, he circled a large patch of brush, ensuring there were no hidden assailants in it. Then he took up a position hidden from the road to wait and watch, as the buckboard approached.

'Got a scout ridin' both sides, stayin' hid,' Red mused. 'If we go after the wagon, they open up from behind us an' cut us down like coyotes.'

'Not a bad plan,' Flint replied.

'Depends which side of it you're on,' Red complained.

Flint frowned in concentration as he studied the actions of all six guards of the precious cargo. He lowered the telescope again. 'Gregorio, are you as good with a knife as Amado is?'

Gregorio grinned. 'Oh, no, Señor Flint. Amado is very much more faster and better.'

'Do not let him lie too much,' Amado disagreed. 'He is very good.'

Flint pursed his lips thoughtfully. 'We gotta get rid o' those outriders, before we can do anything else. If we shoot 'em, it'll alert the ones with the wagon. They'll fort up around the wagon an' we'll have a full-fledged gunfight. No tellin' how we'd come out on that.'

'Yeah, but you got a plan.' Red's voice was as dry as his drawl was slow. 'You always got a plan up yer sleeve.'

Instead of answering directly, Flint said: 'We'll ride up the road till we're a good mile ahead of 'em. Red, you an' Amado will go over ta the other side of the road. Me'n Gregorio'll stay on this side. Pick a spot where that scout will likely stop an' watch for the wagon to catch up. Kill 'im with a knife, if ya can. Don't let his horse get away. If his horse goes runnin' off, they'll likely see it, an' be warned.'

'Wouldn't have to use a knife,' Red offered.

Flint raised his eyebrows. 'No?'

'Not if we're far enough ahead o' the wagon, anyway. If you take your neckerchief an' wrap it around an' around, just at the end o' your gun barrel, it'll muffle the sound so much you won't hear it more'n a hundred yards away.'

'Is that so? I never heard o' that.'

Red nodded. 'I've done it. It works. Works with a feather piller, too. Trouble is, ain't too many folks carry a feather piller 'round with 'em. Everybody's got a neckerchief. 'Course, I also knowed a fella that did it, an' wrapped it too tight. It blowed up his gun barrel. You have to leave it loose enough the bullet ain't blocked.'

Flint thought about it for a long moment, obviously rehearsing the action in his mind. He shrugged. 'Good ta know. You'n me can be ready thataway, just in case the knife don't work with either one. I seen Amado use that knife o' his, though. If he can get close enough without bein' seen, he ain't likely ta miss.'

Amado grinned silently, caressing the handle of the large knife at his belt with his fingertips.

With no further conversation they mounted up. Urging their horses to a swift canter, they rode a wide circle away from the road and nearly two miles along its path. They reined in, as Flint scrambled to the top of a rimrock where he could see the road. He returned in minutes. 'We're a little over a mile ahead of 'em. There's a spot on both sides about a quarter-mile further up, that's perfect for the scouts to ease into an' watch. We'll hide the horses and get into position in both spots on foot, so their horses won't catch wind of ours.'

Again leading the others at a lope, Flint covered the remaining quarter-mile, and found a spot in a deep, brushy arroyo to hide the horses. He pointed out the spot the scouts would almost certainly head for. On both sides of the road a neck of timber came down from taller ridges. The timber ended less than fifty yards from the road on each side. There was no other obvious cover along the road for nearly half a mile.

Quickly each pair moved into the cover of the timber, and took their places where they could see the scouts' approach. They settled down to wait.

Flint and Gregorio chose places about twenty yards apart. Flint could see the wagon, still nearly a mile away. Its team slowed from a trot to a walk, as they began the incline up into the low hills. The scouts emerged from cover, still remaining as close to the same distance from the road as possible, and trotted swiftly forward, scouring the sides of the trail for any sign of ambush.

When they were a quarter-mile away, they waited, sitting their horses in the open. There was no cover there, so they simply sat at a higher elevation than the road, watching the charge they were sent to guard. When the wagon had nearly caught up to them, they turned and trotted on ahead again.

Flint shoved the telescope into itself and laid it at the base of a tree. He removed his neckerchief, wrapping it around the end of the barrel of his Colt Peacemaker. He shoved his finger through the center of it, making sure he could feel the end of the gun barrel. Because the Colt, unlike the Russian .44 on his right hip, still had a front sight, the neckerchief had something to cling to, to keep it in place.

Glancing at Gregorio, he verified the Mexican was alert and watching the scout's approach. He held his knife loosely at his side, appearing totally relaxed.

The scout approached the trees at a trot, not seeming to be concerned that anyone might be waiting within them. He rode just inside their cover and unexpectedly dismounted. Less than ten feet from

Gregorio's hidden position, he turned and watched the approaching wagon for just a moment. Then he undid his trouser fly and began to relieve himself on the ground.

The sound, along with the gunman's diverted attention, was the perfect cover. Gregorio did not hesitate. He stepped forward swiftly and silently three steps. With a swift upward movement, he buried the knife into the base of the gunman's skull. It penetrated more than six inches into the man's brain.

The gunman never felt the blow that felled him. He slumped to the ground, oblivious of his own death. His feet bore witness to the frantic storm of neuron signals the dying brain emitted, as they twitched and jerked. In ten seconds they, too, went still.

Before the gunman's feet had stopped twitching, Gregorio had stepped forward, grabbing the reins of the startled horse. He crooned softly to it, and it settled down quickly. Flint stepped up beside him. 'Nice work, *amigo*,' he complimented.

Gregorio did not answer. He turned away from the horse and jerked his knife from the head of the dead man. He carefully cleaned it with leaves and dry grass, then returned it to its sheath. He looked at Flint, his eyes looking as if the knife were buried in his soul.

All at once the Mexican began to tremble. He sat down on the ground abruptly to keep from falling. He covered his face with his hands. '*Por Dios, por Dios, por Dios*,' he murmured over and over.

Flint laid a hand on his shoulder. 'First man you ever killed?'

Gregorio nodded, beginning to sob. Flint's hand tightened on his shoulder. 'I know how you feel, *amigo*. But you gotta cowboy up. There's trouble headin' our way. I need you backin' me.'

The Mexican lowered his hands. He took a deep breath. He wiped his face on his shirt-sleeve. He stood, carefully avoiding looking at the dead man. 'Forgive me, Señor Flint. I did not know it would feel like this, to kill a man. I did not know. It was so easy to do, and then it was suddenly so terrible a thing. It felt like I, too, died, down deep in my soul some place. And now I am stuck in that place, and it is hard to breathe.'

Flint's voice was hard and flat. 'I know, Gregorio. Now get a grip on yourself. We still got work to do.'

Gregorio crossed himself twice, muttered something softly and took a deep breath. 'Tell me what it is I must do, Señor Flint,' he said.

'The wagon's gettin' close,' Flint instructed at once. 'I'm gonna wear this fella's hat an' ride his horse out in front of 'em, when they're pertneart even. Red'll be watchin'. He'll take the cue from me an' do the same. You steady your rifle on a branch of a tree, where you got a clear field of fire at the road. Aim at the guy on the seat o' the wagon. Not the driver. He'll have the reins in his hands. That'll slow him some. The other one likely has a shotgun. The second anything starts – if you see anyone go for their gun – you shoot that guy. Aim for his belly button. You're higher than the road. If you aim at his

132

chest, you'll likely overshoot. Aim for his belly
button, an' put 'im outa commission. Me'n Red'll
handle the others.'

Gregorio took a deep breath and let it out slowly.
He nodded. '*Sí señor*. I will not miss.'

'I know you won't, *compadre*. I already seen I can
depend on ya.'

Without waiting for an answer, he put the dead
gunman's hat on his own head, retrieved the man's
horse and mounted. He rode to a spot that could be
seen from the timber where Red and Amado should
be waiting, but still concealed from the approaching
wagon, and waved toward the trees on the opposite
side of the road. He spotted movement almost immediately. In half a minute, Red appeared, mounted on
the other outrider's horse.

When he lifted the reins and nudged the horse on
a path to intercept the wagon, Red followed suit.
They were less than half a dozen steps from the trees
when the others spotted them. It took several
seconds for them to realize it was not their own men,
however. By the time they did, both Red and Flint
were less than fifty feet from the wagon.

The driver hauled on the reins, swearing
profusely. The two outriders whipped guns from
their holsters, but they were far, far too slow.

Roaring a fraction of a second apart, both Flint
and Red shot the guards from their saddles. At
almost the same instant, a rifle barked from the trees
on each side of the road. The driver lurched from
the seat of the buckboard, bounced off the front
wheel, and crumpled onto the ground. The guard

133

beside him straightened up, partially lifted from the seat, struggling to raise the double-barreled shotgun in his hands. He collapsed suddenly into a heap without being able to do so.

Flint reached out and grabbed the reins of the closest of the wagon's team of mules, keeping them from running as they were already attempting to do. Under his firm grip they settled down quickly.

Amado from one side, and Gregorio from the other, stepped out of the trees and walked to join the others. 'Now what, Señor Flint?' Amado querried.

Flint ejected the sole expended cartridge from his gun and replaced it with a fresh one. He thought for a minute before answering. 'We best get this team to the closest outfit where we can buy a team o' horses or mules. I don't wanta get charged with horse-stealin'. Then we'll tie the dead men onto their horses, an' the ones from the wagon each onto one o' the mules, an' let 'em go home. They won't likely get there afore tomorrow. By then we'll be well on the way to gettin' that shipment o' sheep an' headin' home with 'em.'

'The gunhands' horses ain't likely from Over-hostlers. They won't know ta go home there.'

'No, but the mules will. The horses'll follow 'em, since they don't have anywhere else ta go.'

Amado said: 'Gregorio, help me to put these two in the back of the wagon. Then we will tie the others onto their horses.'

'We'll put the ones in the trees in the wagon too,' Flint said. 'No sense makin' the horses carry dead men till we have to. They don't like that much.'

134

He couldn't have explained that sudden concern for the horses. He didn't even allow himself to think about it. It wouldn't do at all, for one whose life depended on being as hard as nails, to think he might be softening.

CHAPTER 17

'When did you start goin' soft on them danged stinkin' sheepmen?'

Ulysses J. Hodges, owner of the U-Cross ranch, shrugged. 'I dunno, Gabe. I just been thinkin' a lot. Them sheepmen prob'ly got as much right to open range as we do.'

Gabe Kilmer's face reddened to the point of being almost purple. 'U.J., you know as well as me that cattle won't even touch the grass where them stinkin' things has grazed.'

Hodges shook his head. 'Now I know that ain't true, Gabe. I seen 'em do it. I know the sheep graze the range down shorter, an' they'll eat clear to the roots if they're left too long in one spot, but I been payin' attention. None o' the sheep outfits let their herds do that. They move 'em often enough so they ain't hurtin' the range at all. Why, they even eat some o' them weeds our cows won't eat. I ain't sure but what the range is better off for 'em bein' there.'

Kilmer sputtered, at a loss for words. Finally he shouted: 'Hodges, get off my land! All these years I thought you was a friend. Now you're sidin' with them? With them! If I see you or any o' your hands on my place again, I swear I'll shoot ya like a rabid coyote.'

Hodges didn't move. He sat the saddle, hands folded on the saddle horn, studying his friend. 'You can't kill 'em all, Gabe. Even if it was right ta do it, you just can't kill 'em all. An' that's the only way you could ever get rid of 'em now.'

'I will kill 'em all!' Kilmer raged. 'I got guns comin' to replace the ones we melt the barrels on, an' we'll keep on killin' the danged things till they ain't one o' them stinkin' dang things left standin' in this here country. An' we'll kill every herder that gets in our way doin' it. An' the rest o' the sheepmen, too. An' that high-minded gunfighter o' theirs, too. I got gunfighters just itchin' fer a chance ta show him he ain't so danged good. So do you, Hodges.'

'Your guns ain't comin', Gabe.'

Kilmer stared, open-mouthed, for a brief moment. 'Whatd'ya mean?'

'My mules came home carryin' the gun hands I sent after the guns. Your hands that rode along followed the mules to my place. Well, their horses did.'

'What are you sayin', Hodges?'

'I'm sayin' the sheepmen must have got wind o' the rifles we sent for. They got 'em now, an' we got six more dead gunmen.'

'They got the guns?'

'And all six of our hands that was with 'em are dead, Gabe.'

'Forget the hands. They was just gunfighters

137

anyway. They got our guns?'

'Somebody did.'

'But . . . but . . . well, it don't matter. We got guns enough. Guns and gunfighters. We'll still do it. I still got eight or nine gunfighters on my payroll. So do you.'

Hodges shook his head. 'Not any more, Gabe. I'm lettin' 'em go.'

Kilmer stared in disbelief for several seconds. 'Whatd'ya mean?'

'I mean I'm lettin' all my gun hands go. Those that aren't already dead. I'm goin' back ta just runnin' my ranch. I'm keepin' my cowboys, but I'm lettin' all the gun hands go.'

After several speechless seconds, Kilmer roared: 'Then send 'em over ta me! Tell 'em I'll guarantee 'em two months' wages at a hundred a month an' all the sheep an' Mexicans for target practice they can handle. I'm killin' 'em all, Hodges. I ain't backin' down. I ain't givin' an inch. I'll kill every danged one o' them stinkin' things or die a-tryin'.'

'Well, I ain't gonna stand with you on that, Gabe. Neither is the Rafter-2. Neither is the Flyin' H. Neither is the YL. Neither is the Plum Crick ranch.'

Kilmer stared in disbelief. He swallowed hard. 'You're all desertin'? You're quittin'? You're goin' soft on sheep? I can't believe it. I thought you was all good men an' true. I thought we was in this together.'

Hodges nodded. 'We have been. That's why I rode over today. I don't want you goin' on with this thing, thinkin' everybody's still behind you. I don't know about Mill Iron. I ain't talked to Overhostler. But I do know all the rest have decided we're the ones in the wrong here. We been tryin' to hang onto somethin' that ain't ours to hang onto. We ain't got no more stomach for killin' men nor animals, nor for hirin' others to do our killin' for us. We're lettin' 'em go. We're gonna try to work out somethin' with the sheep outfits to share the range.'

'You can't share the range with sheep!'

'Well, we're gonna try.'

'Not as long as I'm around! You gonna join them greasers an' fight me?'

Hodges shook his head. 'We're not going to fight you, Gabe. But we're not going to back you, neither. We just wanted you to know. If you keep pushin' this thing, you're doin' it alone. Maybe you an' Over-hostler, but none o' the others.'

'You're that afraid o' Flint?'

Hodges turned slightly red. His lips compressed together. 'Gabe, you know me well enough to know I ain't never been afraid o' no man alive. An' even if you have been my friend all these years, I'll not stand for you sayin' maybe I am.'

'Well, that's good,' Kilmer retorted, ' 'cause I just hired on a gun hand that's real itchin' for a chance to stand up to him.'

Hodges' curiosity was piqued. 'Yeah? Who's that?'

'Fella named Blair Stearn. Says he's run into Flint afore, an' he owes 'im. Says he'd buy inta this fracas without pay if he had to, just to get a chance to face Flint.'

'I've heard of 'im. Bad sort. I wouldn't trust him,

even on my own payroll.'

'He's just the sort we need to get rid o' Flint.'

'You knew a couple of Flint's friends have showed up?'

' 'Course I knowed that. Messed up a perfect set-up we had to get rid o' Flint. Ain't gonna make no difference. Stearn'll take care o' Flint. We'll take care o' the rest of 'em. Then we're gonna have us the biggest sheep-shoot this here country ever saw. We're gonna grow grass for our cows that's fertilized an' watered with sheep blood, an' the blood of anyone that gets in our way. That goes for you too, Hodges. An' any U-Cross rider we see, from now on.'

Hodges sighed heavily. 'Well, I'm sorry it's come to this, Gabe. At least we know where we stand.'

He wheeled his horse and trotted from the ranch yard. Kilmer stood in his tracks, glaring at his former friend until he rode out of sight.

CHAPTER 18

Dust filled the air. A seemingly endless procession of railroad cars belched forth bleating sheep until Flint thought the whole country would be too small to hold them.

The yells of herders, the barking of well-trained dogs, the bleating of thousands of sheep, produced a bedlam that threatened to drive him mad. He trotted his horse to a vantage point nearly half a mile away, then watched.

What seemed total chaos to him when he was in the midst of it, became amazingly organized and purposeful from his new perspective. Now he could clearly see the sheep, forty or fifty abreast, following a pair of lead goats. At the commands of their owners, dogs forced hesitant sheep into motion, hazing them together, keeping them moving. Slowly the chaos at the railhead became a moving sea of wool, sweeping like a white tide in the direction of their intended range three days away.

Flint's heart leaped as he recognized a rider loping toward him. Involuntarily, his arm raised and waved back and forth above his head.

He could never in his life remember waving at someone like that. He couldn't bring himself to believe he had just done so. Recognition that Betty had spotted him and was loping her horse toward him simply overcame all his reticence at displaying any emotion. He willed his heart to stop its pounding. It ignored the effort.

Topping the low hill from which he watched, she rode directly to him. Her face was flushed. Her eyes danced. He found himself staring at the full red lips smiling at him, unable to drag his eyes away.

She rode up beside him, her horse facing the opposite way from his, so that they faced each other. She reined her mount to a stop just as their legs touched together. 'Oh, Flint, isn't it just too beautiful for words?' she gushed. 'Aren't they just the most beautiful animals you ever saw? They're in perfect condition! And in three days they'll be on our range.'

'Our range?' he heard himself echo.

Without even being aware of doing so, she laid a hand on his leg. 'Oh, Flint, it's just too wonderful for words. It will bring our herd up to the perfect size to support the ranch. Aren't they just beautiful?'

'You really are,' he said. 'You are so beautiful!'

'What?'

Helpless to stop himself, he reached out an arm and swept her from her saddle. She squealed softly and flung her arms around him to keep from falling as her horse sidled nervously away, leaving her legs dangling in mid air.

She needn't have. He had no intention of letting

142

her fall. He had no intention of letting go of her at all. Ever. He didn't have any intention to kiss her, either. He just did.

Startled at first, she responded with abandon.

He pulled away, suddenly mortified that he had allowed his emotions to control him. 'I . . . I . . . I'm sorry,' he stammered. 'I didn't mean. . . .'

'You better mean it,' she retorted.

He started to reply, but her lips were in the way. They were too soft, too inviting, too demanding. He didn't mind. He surrendered to the reality he had been denying for far too long.

Her weight dangling from their mutual embrace brought her back to reality sooner than she wished. She pulled her head back and looked into his eyes. 'I'd like to stay right here forever, but it's getting awfully uncomfortable,' she said.

He glanced down and realized for the first time that she was dangling in mid air. He felt himself blush for the first time in far too many years. His embarrassment faded almost instantly in the softness of her steady gaze.

'Are you tellin' me you're already uncomfortable with me?' he asked, affecting an artificially exaggerated Southern drawl.

She giggled. 'I'm too uncomfortable to breathe, if you really want to know.'

He leaned sideways in the saddle, lowering her to the ground. She took a deep breath, then looked up into his face. 'Now if you'll get down off that horse maybe we could try that again,' she offered.

He started to dismount when something from the

corner of his eye snapped his attention away from her. 'Somebody's comin',' he said. 'Ridin' hard.'

She followed his gaze. 'Damn!' she exclaimed. 'Couldn't he have been even five minutes later?'

He tore his gaze from the approaching rider. Impulsively he stepped from his horse. 'It'll take him a couple minutes to get here anyway,' he muttered as he reached for her.

They made excellent use of the two minutes.

'I'll catch your horse,' he said, as he pulled away from her embrace.

He pretended not to hear her frustrated sigh as he stepped back into the saddle and caught her horse. He led it back to her, and they trotted together to intercept the approaching rider.

When the horseman spotted them, he veered his course toward them. They stopped, side by side, awaiting his approach.

'That's Bax,' Betty announced quietly.

'Who's Bax?'

'Baxter Campbell. U. J. Hodges' foreman.'

'U-Cross?'

'Uh-huh.'

'Wonder what he's up to.'

'He's a good man, Flint. Honest. I'd hire him in a minute if he'd work sheep.'

Campbell hauled his horse to a stop in a cloud of dust. 'Mornin', Miz Burton. You'd be Flint?'

Flint nodded. 'That's me.'

'My lucky day. Found you both together. The boss sent me to talk to you.'

'Hodges?'

144

'Uh-huh. He wants to let you know that him an' most o' the other ranchers have backed off.'

'Backed off?'

'They . . . well, Hodges anyway . . . I 'spect he's speakin' fer the others too . . . they figgered out we been in the wrong, tryin' to run all you sheep outfits outa the country. The country's big enough fer all of us. When ya get back with them woolies yer herdin', they'd like a chance ta palaver.'

Betty's eyes jerked to Flint. They brimmed with moisture, threatening to spill over. Flint's eyes were flat and hard. 'All of 'em?' he demanded.

Campbell shook his head. 'Not Kilmer. Maybe not Overhostler. Don't know about him. All the others, though.'

'So we're only goin' up against one outfit now, maybe two?'

'That's about the size of it. Yer a long way from home free, though.'

'Whatd'ya mean?'

'Well, my outfit . . . The U-Cross . . . we done let all our gun hands go. So'd the other outfits, except the two I mentioned. You still got 'em ta deal with, though.'

'Why?'

'Cuz Kilmer put out the word that he'd hire all of 'em we canned. Offerin' 'em two months' pay guaranteed. Hundred a month.'

Flint and Betty exchanged glances. The brimming joy in her eyes turned to worry and fear.

'What's he got planned?' Flint demanded.

'Don't know,' Campbell replied. 'Don't know as I

145

could say if I did know. I'm still a cowman. I wouldn't feel right ta back-stab another cow outfit, even if they are in the wrong. We jist wanted ya to know it's betwixt you an' Kilmer, an' maybe Overhostler, whatever happens. The rest of us ain't in it.'

Flint digested the information a long moment, then nodded curtly. 'Much obliged.'

Without waiting for anything more, Campbell wheeled his horse and rode away at a swift trot. 'Thanks, Bax,' Betty called after him.

Without turning, Campbell lifted a hand in farewell.

'What do we do now, honey,' Betty asked softly.

The term of endearment jarred Flint. He had been called a lot of things, but never that. Well, not by anyone like Betty. He forced himself to concentrate on the situation at hand, terrified suddenly that his attention was so divided. He welcomed the focus another approaching rider forced upon him.

'Someone else comin',' he announced.

'Oh! Now what?'

'Reg'lar parade today.'

'It's Amado.'

Flint nodded with satisfaction. 'He oughta have some word of what Kilmer's up to.'

'I hope so. Andy wasn't too happy about not having him to help unload the sheep.'

'There's lots o' herders. Not just yours. You got sheep there for six ranches.'

'Ours,' she corrected.

'What?'

'Not just ours. I want them to be ours. Not mine.'

146

He pushed the thought aside. 'Let's deal with one thing at a time,' he insisted.

She acted as if to answer, then turned her attention instead to Amado's approach. Unlike Campbell, he rode at a trot, seemingly in no hurry.

'You don't seem too excited, but I 'spect you must have some news,' Flint observed.

Amado grinned. '*Sí, señor.* Señora Burton. I do not see why that I should ride my horse to death to tell you what you do not need to know until tomorrow.'

Flint glared silently, impatiently, waiting for him to continue. Betty was unable to do the same. 'So what did you find out, Amado?'

'There has been a big split in the ranchers,' he announced. 'Most of the cow ranches have said they do not wish to fight any more with us.'

'But what about the ones that do?' Flint demanded.

Amado's grin faded. 'That is the bad news, Señor Flint. All of the gunfighters that the other ranchers have fired have been hired right back by Señor Kilmer.'

Flint's response was brittle. 'So we're facin' just as many gunmen as we were.'

'Well, *sí* and *no*,' Amado said. 'Now it is only the gunfighters. The cowboys are taking care of cattles and not part of what the others are getting ready to do.'

'So get to what they're planning,' Flint demanded.

'*Sí.* I am coming to that. Do you know the place called Denton Spring?'

Flint nodded. 'It's just the other side of a long

147

valley, where it opens out into several square miles of good grass.'

'*Sí*. That long valley just before the spring, it is, oh, maybe three hundred yards across most of the way. On both sides it has rocky slopes going up, like the walls.'

'I noticed it. Good place for an ambush.'

'*Sí*. That is exactly the plan of the Circle-J, and maybe the Mill Iron, I could not find out for sure. They plan to have all of their gunfighters in those rocks on both sides of that valley. They can shoot from there to past the middle. It is their plan to hide in the rocks there until all of us and all of the sheeps are in that valley, and then to begin shooting. They plan to kill all of us, then to shoot all of our sheeps.'

Betty gasped. 'They plan to shoot six thousand sheep?'

Amado nodded. '*Sí*. That is what Señor Flint already figured out was the plan, so that they had bought all the rifles we took from them. Without those rifles, they will make the barrels of their rifles melt with so much shooting, but they will kill them all just the same.'

'Unless we spoil the party,' Flint said.

Amado grinned. '*Sí*. It is a party I am looking forward to spoiling *muy mucho*.'

Betty's eyes bored into Flint. 'What are we going to do?'

Flint ignored her for the moment. 'What about the rest of the ranchers?'

'*Sí*. I find them too. There is a small place a few

miles the other side of the Denton Spring. It is called Sage Flats.'

'I know the place. One saloon and wh. . . . Uh, one saloon's 'bout all that's there.'

Amado grinned broadly at Flint's discomfiture. '*Sí.* It is there that some men of the ranches wait to talk with us. They think the Circle-J will not stop us. I think they believe in Señor Flint more than they believe in Señor Kilmer.'

'Well, let's see what we can do to make sure they're right. Betty, how many of these herders will it take to control the sheep, once they're all lined out?'

She studied his eyes, seeking something to allay her fears. 'Less than half of them. There are, I think, thirty-eight or forty herders all together, from all the ranches that have sheep here.'

'So I could take twenty of them without a problem?'

'Well, yes.'

Nodding with satisfaction, he began to explain the plan unfolding in his mind.

CHAPTER 19

An eagle soared silently, riding a thermal updraft, watching the stream below. Abruptly it folded its wings and dove, plummeting earthward. Twenty feet above the stream it spread its wings, swooped low over the water of a shallow pool, and plucked a plump rainbow trout from a riffle. With a steady beat of mighty wings it bore the thrashing fish skyward, toward its eyrie and the hungry mouths awaiting.

A dust devil erupted amongst scrub sage, whirling dust and dry grass into the air, then dropping its collection of debris as it faded from existence.

A horse snorted softly and stamped a foot to dislodge a biting fly, then idly swished more of the pests away with its tail. Tethered amongst more than a dozen of its fellows, it waited patiently the return of its rider.

Flint dismounted, motioning the ten others to do likewise. Some of them did so smoothly, easily. Others did so awkwardly, unused to handling a rifle and a horse at the same time. They tied their horses in close proximity to those already there.

Moving swiftly and quietly, he approached the

crest of the hill ahead of them. In the distance he could hear the bleating of the sheep, punctuated regularly by the sharp bark of a dog, or a command, usually in Spanish, to one of the dogs.

Glancing back that way, he could see the cloud of dust the approaching ovine sea stirred into the late morning air.

At the crest of the rise, just before the ground fell away in a rocky slope to the valley below, Flint motioned to those following him to get down and stay put. He crept forward on all fours, then on his belly, until he could see the boulder-strewn descent. Clearly exposed below him, Gabe Kilmer and more than a dozen of his gunfighters were nestled behind rocks, waiting, rifles settled onto stony rests.

Beside each gunman lay at least one extra rifle and several boxes of cartridges. Glancing up, Flint caught a glimpse of movement on the crest of the opposite hill. Watching, he soon spotted Red Saxon, in a position exactly corresponding to his own, surveying those hidden in the rocks bounding the valley on that side.

He slid carefully, silently backward, until he could motion with no danger of being detected by the waiting gunmen. Then he turned. Silently he held up four fingers, and motioned to his left. Six fingers and a motion to his right sent the rest of his men that direction. When they had moved to a single-file line to either side of him, he motioned them farther away, lengthening the line to correspond to the positions of the would-be bushwhackers.

When they were all in the position he indicated,

he motioned them forward. They crept up to the crest of the hill, then turned to grin at one another in the realization that the enemy was pinned helplessly before and below them.

There was no way Kilmer and his men could escape. Two of the herders on each side were armed with 50-caliber Sharps rifles, which could reach the far slope easily. If the gunmen moved to the side of the boulders that protected them from the force ranged above, they would be in plain sight of those on the far crest. The hunters' perfect trap now made them perfect prey.

Watching the crest of the far side of the valley, Flint waited until Red's force was in a similar configuration. Then he stood. Instantly, Red stood up on the far slope. At that signal, all of the herders except the ones armed with the Sharps also stood, forming a line above the gunfighters on both sides.

Gunfighters noticed the line on the far side of the valley first. A shouted warning was followed by a chorus of similar warnings. As if controlled by a single impulse, each whirled to see the line of rifles aimed from above at his own position.

Time suspended as silently as the lonely eagle riding the thermal. Just as suddenly as the bird had plummeted earthward toward its prey, the slopes of the valley exploded with sound.

It was impossible, either then or later, to know who fired the first shot. One of the gunmen, probably by well-honed instinct, saw the threat and reacted with practiced response. It only took one shot to ignite the firestorm.

Half of the gunmen fell in the first fusillade. Several scrambled around a boulder, only to die with the impact of a 50-caliber shell from the far bank, or to have one such splatter the rocks close enough to send them scrambling back into the withering fire from above.

Swearing furiously, Gabe Kilmer killed one herder and missed another before several bullets forever ended his mad vendetta against everything connected with sheep.

On the far side of the valley, Milton Overhostler immediately perceived the hopelessness of the situation. He threw down his gun, raised his hands, and yelled at the top of his voice: 'Give it up, boys! Throw down your guns! They got us dead to rights.'

Addressing the top of the hill he hollered; 'Don't shoot! We give up.'

Somehow, even among the hail of lead and roar of rifles, his voice carried and prevailed. The din stilled. Silence settled like the debris of a dying dust devil.

Even the survivors on Flint's side of the valley complied, dropping their weapons and raising their hands.

In swift order, the surviving gunmen were herded to the bottom of the valley and stripped of their remaining weapons. Overhostler walked to a small boulder, sat down on it, rested his elbows on his knees and hung his head. He sat motionless as orders were issued to herders who retrieved the gunmen's horses. When the horses arrived, Flint had each searched for additional weapons. When they were removed and piled to one side, he spoke.

'I ain't sure why, but I'm givin' you boys one more chance to get out o' this deal alive. Any of you that give your word to ride out an' keep ridin' till you're clear o' Wyoming, can mount your horse and ride. But do it quick.'

He didn't need to extend the offer twice. One gunman, wounded, needed help to get into the saddle. In fifteen minutes they were all gone out of sight.

Flint turned to Overhostler. 'What about you?' he demanded.

For the first time since collapsing onto the rock, Overhostler raised his head. 'I guess that's up to you. I'm whipped.'

'What you do ain't up to me to decide,' Flint disagreed. 'If bein' whipped means you're willin' to live an' let live with the sheepmen, then you best head fer home. You got a ranch to run.'

Overhostler studied the legendary gunman for a long moment. 'You'd just let me ride out o' here? Go home an' act like nothin' happened? Go home an' pretend I didn't try to kill all of you an' your sheep as well?'

'If you give me your word it's over, that's exactly what I'll do.'

'I had you figured for bein' hard as nails.'

'I can be. Have been, mostly. I ain't never killed anybody I didn't need to, to do my job.'

'I ain't likely to ever be able to stand bein' around sheep or sheep people.'

'Nobody's askin' you to. No sheepmen are gonna show up on your doorstep wantin' to be friends with

154

you, neither. You kin live an' let live, all the same.'

After a long silence Overhostler rose to his feet. 'I can do that,' he agreed. 'The rest o' the ranchers is waitin' for ya at Sage Brush Flats. They had it figgered that you was a better man than me, an' you'd ride outa here in one piece. They wanta work out some kinda agreement on use o' the range. Whatever you work out with them, I'll abide by.'

'Fair enough,' Flint agreed.

Overhostler started to mount his horse, then stopped and walked to Flint. Silently he held out a hand. Flint took it, returning the solid grip. Without a word the rancher mounted his horse and loped from the valley.

CHAPTER 20

A Hog Ranch, it was called, usually. Sage Brush Flats seemed too pretentious. A saloon too dirty to exist anywhere else offered watered whiskey and cheap rye. Three or four whores, too old, or too ugly, or too disease-ridden to solicit any better clientele survived on the desperate loneliness of drifters and soldiers condemned to duty at the nearby fort. Even that fort was sparsely manned and all but forgotten by its own army.

A ragged corral and clapboard barn provided meager shelter for the horses of the saloon's patrons during the harsh winters. There were two occupied shacks rounding out the entire pretense of a town.

From a distance, Flint and Red sized up the terrain. Neither could see the gunman stretched flat on the saloon's roof, rifle pointed, waiting patiently. He stationed Andres 300 yards from the saloon, on the crest of a rise, with one of the Sharps rifles. On another rise, shielded by scattered rocks, he stationed Amado with another Sharps. 'You boys cover us from here,' he said.

The two of them, with Andy Sparks and Ian

Flanders, rode forward to their rendezvous with the ranchers.

There were 250 yards to go.

Flint's eyes darted everywhere, still leery of the possibility of a trap.

There were still 200 yards.

Nothing moved. He counted ten horses tied up to the rails of the corral. All saddled. Ten men. Three bore army issue, A-frame saddles. Seven ranchers. Seven to four. Seven to six in the open, where Andres and Amado could back them.

He knew at once he would not enter the saloon for the meeting with the ranchers. He would call them out, meet them in the open, where it would be less of an advantage to the first on the scene.

Still 150 yards.

The artificial sound of a woman's contrived laughter drifted from the saloon. The trigger-finger of the gunman on the roof tightened slightly.

One hundred yards.

Subconsciously Flint noted the brands on the horses. Rafter-2. B-Bar-C. U-Cross. Flying H. YL. Mill Iron.

Mill Iron. Overhostler. He's here ahead of us. They already know all about the trap not workin'. Horse is still sweatin' pretty good. Ain't sure whether it's good or bad he's here.

Fifty yards.

Faintly, behind them, he heard the pounding of the hoofs of a running horse. He jerked his own horse to a stop and turned.

'Somebody in an awful hurry,' he muttered.

'Ridin' flat out.'

His horse sidestepped nervously, bumping another horse, then shifting back the other way. The hidden gunman swore softly, trying to line up his sights on Flint's chest.

'It's Betty!' he said.

He stepped from his horse and walked away from the others, staring at the approaching woman. She was flattened across her saddle horn, lashing her horse with every stride, yelling something at the top of her voice. He could hear the voice, but couldn't understand anything.

The others had dismounted as well. They clustered behind him, muttering to themselves, hands on guns, each fighting down his own sense of impending danger. Their movement continually interfered with the concealed sniper having a clean shot. Patiently, he held a bead on Flint and waited.

Betty didn't slow the horse as she approached. He heard her scream: 'Flint! Look out! Blair Stearn is here somewhere!'

She lunged from her horse, flying to Flint's arms. He caught her, spinning to slow her to a stop and retain his balance. Her panic-stricken gaze wrenched his heart as she tried to control her emotions enough to speak.

'Flint! Flint! There's a man after you. His name is Stearn. One of the gunfighters told a herder to let you know. He's going to kill. . . .'

As he caught her, for the first time none of the others was between Flint and Sage Brush Flats. For an instant his back was completely exposed. As her

158

speed and weight forced him to swing around, it was Betty who was there.

She jerked against him and grunted. In the ensuing instant the roar of a rifle reached his ears. He knew instantly, with sickening certainty she had taken the bullet meant for him.

He threw her to the ground, covering her with his own body. His Colt Peacemaker was in his hand, searching for a target.

On the flat roof of the saloon a man stood up suddenly, propelled backward. Flint fired twice before he realized someone else had already shot the sniper. The bark of a Sharps 50 finally reached him from Andres' rifle.

He jammed the Colt back into its holster and turned his attention to Betty. Heedless of anything except her, he whipped a knife from its sheath and began to cut away the blood-soaked cloth of the back of her dress.

She groaned. It was the most beautiful sound he had ever heard. Using part of the dress he had cut away, he swiped frantically at the welling blood, exposing the wound. Stearn's bullet had hit her shoulder-blade at an angle as he'd whirled her around. It glanced from the bone, tearing a gash across the back of her shoulder, but penetrating no farther. His heart soared.

Elated, he wadded cloth into the wound to stanch the blood, and turned her over, cradling her in his arms.

Her eyes focused on him. 'What happened?' she asked. 'Something hit me.'

159

Flint's words were much more matter-of-fact than he felt. 'You got shot.'

Her eyes clouded. 'Am I . . . is it . . . am I going to die?'

'Nope.' He grinned. Her world exploded in sunshine as the first grin she had seen on him spread across his face. 'Not a chance. You're gonna be just fine. You're gonna be fine enough that you an' me is gonna make enough little Flints to gravel the whole yard.'

She knew she'd like that idea, just as soon as her shoulder stopped hurting.